His love will last unti[l]
the end of time...

D0036406

MY LORD
IMMORTALITY

DEBBIE RALEIGH

ZEBRA
U.S.$4.99
CAN $6.99

FEELING WICKED

His fingers moved to trace the line of her brow, sending a shock of sensation through her body. "Nights such as this lead to all sorts of wicked thoughts."

Wicked. Amelia shivered, feeling oddly unlike herself in the darkened garden. Perhaps it was the moonlight. Or the delicious scent of roses. Or perhaps this was simply a moment out of time, she thought dizzily. Whatever the reason, she desperately longed to shrug aside her heavy burdens and responsibilities. Just for now she wanted to be a young, beautiful maiden with nothing to concern her but a very desirable flirtation with a handsome gentleman.

"You intrigue me, sir. What possible wicked thoughts could a gentleman such as you possess?"

His breath rasped through the air at her deliberately provoking manner, but his expression never altered.

"Thoughts best forgotten, my dear."

"Why?"

"You do enjoy playing with fire, do you not?" he murmured, his fingers moving to outline the full curve of her lips. . . .

Books by Debbie Raleigh

Published by Zebra Books

MY LORD
IMMORTALITY

Debbie Raleigh

ZEBRA BOOKS
Kensington Publishing Corp.
http://www.kensingtonbooks.com

ZEBRA BOOKS are published by

Kensington Publishing Corp.
850 Third Avenue
New York, NY 10022

All Kensington titles, imprints and distributed lines are available at special quantity discounts for bulk purchases for sales promotion, premiums, fund-raising, educational or institutional use.

Special book excerpts or customized printings can also be created to fit specific needs. For details, write or phone the office of the Kensington Special Sales Manager: Kensington Publishing Corp., 850 Third Avenue, New York, NY 10022. Attn. Special Sales Department. Phone: 1-800-221-2647.

Zebra and the Z logo Reg. U.S. Pat. & TM Off.

First Printing: December 2003
10 9 8 7 6 5 4 3 2 1

Printed in the United States of America

Prologue

The cottage set in the thick copse of trees was a dark, cramped affair. Abandoned years before, it had been forgotten by all but the spiders and an occasional rat. Even the air was stale with a thick dust that threatened to choke the unwary.

On this moonless night, however, the rats and spiders had been driven from the darkness. Not even those shadowy creatures could dare the cold mist of fog that slowly, ruthlessly seeped through the door.

Drake Ramone suppressed a delicate shudder as he watched the mist swirl ever closer. As a vampire of considerable power, he feared nothing. Why should he?

He was destined for greatness. Both upon this dreary mortal plane and behind the Veil that currently protected the vampires from his wrath. It was his undoubted birthright.

Still, he discovered a vague sense of unease as the fog thickened. His power was not as formidable as this ancient vampire. Not yet. Until he held the Medallion in his hands he would have to remain an unwilling servant to his master.

"Drake," the mist whispered in steely tones.

"Welcome, Master," he murmured with a low bow. "You honor me with your presence."

There was a grating laugh that echoed eerily through the barren cottage. "Honor? Do you believe me a fool? You honor no one, Drake," the vampire sneered.

"Perhaps not." Drake gave an indifferent shrug. "But I have always honored power."

"No, you lust after power."

"Surely it is one and the same?"

"To honor implies you possess a measure of principles. A tedious weakness that has never troubled you."

Drake offered a tight smile. "Certainly not."

"Which is precisely why you were chosen. Only one with your arrogant ambition would be willing to steal the Medallion and bring an end to the Veil."

"It is our mutual ambition, I believe."

"Yes." There was a pause, as if the elder were searching Drake's black heart. And perhaps he was, as he gave a dry rasp. "But do not allow that ambition to be your downfall. I sense your burning desires. If you betray me I will crush you beneath my heel."

Drake restrained his temper with an effort. When the vampire had first approached him behind the Veil he had been reluctant to agree to his scheme. He was an Immortal. A true blood. He took commands from no one. But as he pondered the rewards that could be his, his reluctance had faded.

It had been nearly two hundred years ago that the greatest of all vampires, Nefri, had created the Veil. She had commanded that the vampires live apart from humans. It was for the good of all, she had claimed, that the vampires exist in seclusion to ponder the great truths and philosophies. They were abruptly separated from the mortal world. The bloodlust that had once made them vulnerable to sunlight and fire had been wrenched from their souls.

Without human blood, however, they had also lost the desire, the lust and hungers, of humans. They lost their ancient powers. The ability to shape-shift and mist-walk. They lost their fierce need to hunt.

For Drake it was an unbearable existence. He was no cold, passionless scholar who desired to devote an eternity to seeking a higher existence. He did not wish the knowledge of the elders.

What he wanted was to compel others to his command. He wanted to crush and enslave the humans, and to feast upon their blood. He wanted the other vampires to bend to his will.

An impossible task as long as Nefri held the ancient Medallion that kept the Veil in place.

So, along with Tristan and Amadeus, he had allowed himself to be secretly slipped through the Veil. They had returned to the world of mortals to discover Nefri and take the Medallion from her grasp.

None of them could have suspected that the wily old vampire would choose to separate the Medallion into three amulets, or that she would soul-bind them to mortal women.

Suddenly the Medallion could not be taken by force or even death. The mortals must give the amulets of their free will, or the power within them would be destroyed.

It had been a clever ploy. Even Drake had to admit that much. But that did not halt his seething determination. He would have the Medallion. No matter what he must do.

And once he did, all would suffer beneath his power.

Including this arrogant, treacherous vampire who chided him as if he were a hapless minion.

"I seek only to retrieve the Medallion as you requested, Master," he forced himself to retort, his thin countenance wreathed with a chilled smile. "No more."

The mist swirled. "We shall see. Have you discovered the wench?"

"Yes. I managed to rent a town house within the same block as Miss Hadwell. I have even managed to make contact with her brother, a rather pathetic half-wit. I hope to use the boy to get closer to the maiden."

"And Sebastian?"

Drake curled his lips at the mention of the vampire who had been sent by the Great Council to force him to return to the Veil.

"The fool has taken a house a few blocks away. He poses no threat, however. As usual, he is impervious to all but his musty books and ancient studies. He has not even made an attempt to seek me out. When he does, I shall kill him and be done."

There was a dry hiss of disapproval at his flippant tone. "He is there because I swayed the Council to choose him. Just as I chose that tediously noble Gideon and that vain fool Lucien. I presumed that they would easily be defeated. Just as I chose my servants because I presumed they possessed the necessary intelligence and lust to conquer. A miscalculation that I now must rue."

Drake frowned. "What are you implying?"

"Tristan has been destroyed, along with Amadeus. You alone are left."

Drake felt the chill seep to his bones. While he considered the two vampires who had joined him in the battle to destroy the Veil beneath contempt, he could not deny a vague sense of shock.

"How?"

"In their arrogance they thought they could not be defeated. The same arrogance that you carry about you, Drake."

The handsome features surrounded by a short crop

of golden curls hardened at the insult. Tristan and Amadeus were pathetic idiots when compared to him.

"Sebastian is no match for me."

"He possesses the dagger."

Drake shrugged. Although the dagger given to Sebastian had been blessed with ancient power to destroy a vampire, he remained unimpressed. The reclusive scholar was no threat. Not to a vampire destined to rule all.

"Sebastian will soon be at an end. And once I have the amulet from Miss Hadwell, I will seek out the others. Soon enough, the Medallion will be mine."

"I believe you mean *ours*," that rasping voice reminded him.

"Ah, yes. Of course."

Without warning, the mist struck out, cutting a thin wound along Drake's cheek. Just as swiftly, it wrapped about the vampire's feet and with a thrust had him tumbling to the dust-covered floor.

"You seek to rise above yourself, Drake. A deadly mistake," the elder warned. "I will have the Medallion. You can rule beneath me or join Tristan and Amadeus in oblivion. The choice is yours."

Wisely remaining upon the hard floor despite the fury that raged through him, Drake patiently waited for the mist to slowly swirl toward the door. It was only then that he raised a hand to touch the blood freely flowing down his face.

Soon, he reassured his savaged pride. Soon he would have the Medallion. Then he would crush all those who had dared to stand in his way.

Beginning with Sebastian St. Ives.

One

The old Gypsy was huddled upon the filthy street like a bundle of forgotten rags. Amelia had nearly passed her by when the woman had abruptly held out her hand in a desperate motion.

"Please, kind lady, will you help me?"

Amelia hesitated. The streets near St. Giles were littered with such pathetic outcasts. Thieves, whores, and the dredges of society waged a daily battle with survival. It was an impossible task to help them all.

The sensible choice was to be about her business so she could return to the comfort of her home. To linger would only invite danger. Especially to a young woman on her own.

Amelia's heart, however, was never sensible. Reaching into her basket, she pulled out the apples and cheese that she had so recently purchased and gently placed them beside the old woman.

"Here you are. Fresh from the market."

"Bless you," the Gypsy murmured. "Bless you."

"And here is a guinea. Sleep well tonight, my dear."

"Ah, so kind." The woman reached for the coin, and then, without warning, she pressed a heavy object into Amelia's hand. "Such generosity must be rewarded."

"Oh . . ." Startled, Amelia regarded the golden amulet that sparkled in the palm of her hand. It was *oddly designed with faint words scratched upon the metal.* "No, you cannot part with such a lovely piece of jewelry. It must be worth a great deal."

The Gypsy slowly smiled. "It is beyond price. As is the blessing that has been placed upon it."

"Then certainly you must keep it. You have more need than I."

"No." A sadness touched the wrinkled countenance. "Darkness will soon stalk you, my dear. A terrible darkness. This amulet will protect you and bring a Guardian to your side. Wear it always and, above all, never give it to another."

Amelia gave a shake of her head. The poor woman was obviously daft. "I cannot keep such a gift."

A gnarled hand reached out to firmly fold Amelia's fingers over the amulet. At the same moment, a strange warmth flared between them.

"It is now bound to you. Protect it well. Only you can halt the danger that threatens all of London. A danger that is drawing ever closer."

Amelia frowned as a chill spread through her body. Daft or not, the old woman was beginning to frighten her.

"Danger? What danger?"

"Keep the amulet close. And trust in your heart. Love is always the light that will hold back the darkness."

"I do not understand." Amelia stepped closer, but even as she did, the old woman was fading into a shimmering mist. A sense of panic clutched at Amelia's heart. "Wait. You must tell me. What danger? Tell me . . ."

A sharp noise echoed through the silent house.

With a sudden wrench, Amelia sat upright in her bed and glanced about the dark chamber. What was it?

Something had awakened her, she realized, as her hand instinctively went to the Medallion on a chain about her neck. Something other than the dream. A dream that had plagued her since the peculiar encounter with the old Gypsy nearly a month ago.

For a moment she hesitated. It was late. Very late. Then, with a resigned sigh she slipped from the bed and pulled a wrap over her nightrail. There was little use in giving in to the desire to lie back and curl up beneath her covers. She would not be able to sleep until she had assured herself that all was well. It was her duty now that she was mistress of her own household.

A faint smile touched her delicate features as she left the bedchamber and moved down the narrow hall. It was not much of a household to boast of. The house was a modest establishment perched upon the shabby fringes of London's more elegant neighborhoods. The rooms were cramped with well-worn furnishings and the garden so small that the handful of roses she had planted threatened to overwhelm it.

Still, it was ample for her and her younger brother, William. Together with their housekeeper, Mrs. Benson, they rubbed along reasonably well.

Pausing at the end of the hall, Amelia fumbled to light a candle before continuing down the stairs and toward the back of the house. A heavy silence shrouded her as she peered into the shadows. In the flickering candlelight everything appeared to be in order, but she instinctively continued her search into the kitchen.

Something had awakened her. A noise that had warned her that someone was stirring despite the late hour.

Refusing to consider the notion that the noise might have been a rat or some other vile creature, she skirted the large table and moved toward the laundry room. It was then that a movement outside the window suddenly caught her attention. William, she realized as she watched the shadowed form crossing the garden. With a hurried movement she rushed toward the door and threw it open.

As swift as she was, however, she was too late to halt her brother as he dashed from the back of the garden in obvious pursuit of his recently acquired cat.

"Bloody hell," Amelia muttered beneath her breath.

What the devil was William thinking? She had specifically warned him not to leave the house without her or Mrs. Benson at his side. She had even made him pledge in words that not even he could fail to understand.

Certainly he knew better than to go out in the middle of the night.

Amelia pushed her hands impatiently through the heavy strands of her raven hair. Calm yourself, she commanded as she sucked in a deep breath. Becoming rattled would serve nothing. William was not attempting to defy her wishes; he simply did not understand.

And why should he? Since she had taken the small house, she had allowed her brother to come and go as he pleased. For the first time in his eighteen years he was not hidden in his chamber nor treated as a source of embarrassment to be tucked away. She had encouraged him to seek out friends among the neighbors and to spend his days among those unfortunate children in the stews who had swiftly learned to love his simple kindness and, perhaps more important, the numerous treats he would bring with him.

It was little wonder he found it difficult to return to his life of being treated as a prisoner. He could not comprehend the danger that suddenly stalked the streets of St. Giles. To him the sudden deaths of the prostitutes were a source of deep sadness, but not a direct threat. His heart was far too tender and without guile to ever consider the notion of someone desiring to harm him.

Once again in command of her nerves, Amelia reached for a cloak that hung by the door and wrapped it tightly about her. There was simply nothing to do but go after William. She certainly could not allow him to wander the streets when there was a madman on the loose.

Ignoring the stones that dug into her bare feet, she stepped into the garden and hurried toward the back gate. The heaviness in the air warned that soon a thick fog would be rolling in, and she grimaced. There were few things more unpleasant than London streets at night.

Wrapping the cloak tighter, she heaved a small sigh. It was not that she regretted leaving her parents' grand town house in the center of Mayfair. Nor giving up the lavish lifestyle that had been her birthright. Oh, granted she enjoyed frivolous entertainments and the flirtations of handsome dandies as much as the next young maiden, but it was a shallow pleasure when placed next to the happiness of her brother. And after learning of her mother's determination to have poor William secretly placed in Bedlam, she had known she had to take matters into her own hands.

No one would be allowed to put William in that horrid place. Perhaps he was dull-witted, and at times rather odd. And there could be no doubt he was inclined to wander off without regard to himself or those who fretted over him. But he was not daft. Nor was he a danger to others.

Still, she had to admit that there were times when she felt the burden of caring for William more heavily than others. Times such as this.

She held the candle high as she entered the small

lane that lay beyond her garden, careful to avoid the inevitable rubbish that was carelessly tossed about. Ahead she could hear the shuffle of footsteps and she hurried her pace. The sooner she caught up to William, the sooner she could return to her bed.

Unfortunately, no matter how swiftly she attempted to make her way through the shadows, she could not catch her brother's far longer strides. Muttering a curse, she passed by the darkened houses, her poor feet protesting her maltreatment. On and on she went. Past one street and then another. It was not until she was near the derelict stables that had been left abandoned years ago that she heard a sound of scuffling and came to an abrupt halt.

At last.

Peering through an overgrown hedge, Amelia was able to faintly make out a shadowed shape. It had to be William. Who else would be skulking in the alley at this time of night? But then the shadow shifted and her relief was swiftly smothered. There was a fluid stealth to the shadow that was nothing at all like William's clumsy movements.

She leaned forward, attempting to determine the exact nature of the shadow, only to feel her heart come to a halt.

There was something wrong. Something terribly wrong.

Even from a distance she could sense a dark, smoldering malice. It was in the unnatural chill in the air. In the thick silence that was nearly choking.

And there was a smell . . . a smell of cold steel shared with something far more foul.

Prickles of alarm raced down her spine as she heedlessly dropped the candle. She should flee, a voice warned from the back of her mind. Whatever was in the shadows was evil. And dangerous. She had to leave before it could turn the malignant attention in her direction.

A wise decision, no doubt. Unfortunately, it had barely formed in her mind when the shadow stilled and then slowly shifted toward her frozen form.

"Who is there?" a voice hissed.

Amelia bit her bottom lip to keep herself from squeaking in startled alarm. Through the hedge it appeared that the shadow was . . . formless. As though it flowed and shifted like mercury upon water. It had to be a trick of the moonlight, she tried to reassure herself. Shapeless shadows did not exist except in children's nightmares. Not even on the narrow, mean streets of London.

Then the shadow once again shifted and, unbelievably, Amelia's horror only deepened. There was something on the ground. A body, she slowly realized. A body that was not moving and that was covered in a dark, ghastly dampness that she very much feared was blood.

Dear heavens, she had to get away.

"I feel you," the shadow rasped in a hollow voice. "I smell your lovely, warm blood. Come to me. Come and offer yourself to me."

A faint tingle raced through Amelia at the command. Almost as if the words held a strange power. But even as her mind seemed to cloud, there was a sharp stab of warmth that seared against her skin. Her trembling fingers lifted to touch the amulet about her neck. It was hot to the touch, and strangely comforting.

The shadow, however, appeared to shrink as she grimly held onto the Medallion, a steely hiss echoing through the air.

"You." Slowly, steadily the shadow grew larger, leeching its way toward the hedge. "Come to me."

"No," Amelia whispered, forcing her shaky legs to take a step backward.

"Do not fear. I will not harm you. Come."

Amelia froze. What was this thing? Nothing human, surely? A thing of nightmares. Of horror stories.

A sob was wrenched from her throat, but even as the shadow neared, there was a sudden flurry of movement from behind the shadow. In less than the beat of a heart, a large, utterly solid form had blocked the path between her and the advancing danger.

A form that thankfully appeared to be human.

"Halt." The new form held up an arm and Amelia could see the glint of a sharp blade in the silver moonlight. "I will not allow this."

A dark, grating laugh echoed through the silence. *"You?* You will not allow?"

Amelia's rescuer never wavered. "No."

"Do not be more of a fool than you need to be. Return to your books and pathetic studies. You do not possess the courage nor the will to confront me."

"Shall we see? Shall we test the strength of my dagger? I do not fear you."

Lost in a thick fog of terror, Amelia nevertheless managed to notice that the gentleman now standing between her and the shadow was surprisingly large. Not only tall, but broad through the shoulders and possessing the type of chiseled muscles not often seen in society.

She also realized that his rich, smoky tones held a trace of an accent that was impossible to trace.

Not that she particularly cared if he were a foreigner or not, she acknowledged with a near-hysterical urge to laugh. At the moment she would have welcomed the devil himself if he were here to protect her.

The shadow seemed to swirl, then, with a sudden hiss, it slowly began to retreat toward the nearby stables.

"We will settle this later, fool. I must think how best to punish you for your insolence," the shadow warned before it disappeared entirely.

For a breathless moment there was nothing but the thick silence; then, with a flowing swiftness that was oddly similar to that of the deadly shadow, the gentleman turned and threaded his way through the thick hedge. Amelia regarded him with a sense of lingering shock, not even flinching when he reached out to gently touch her hair.

"Are you harmed?" he demanded in soft tones.

Amelia struggled to breathe as she pressed a hand to her painfully racing heart. "No. I . . . what was that thing?"

He seemed to hesitate. "A creature. A creature of the dark."

"Creature?" Amelia gave a sudden shudder. Did he mean an animal? No. She had seen what she had seen. That had been something other than human or animal. "What sort of creature?"

Without warning, he reached out to grasp her arm in a firm grip. "Come, we must not linger here."

Before she even knew what was happening, Amelia discovered herself being tugged away from the hedge and turned back down the alley toward her home. Just for a moment, she allowed herself to follow his lead, wanting nothing more than to be back in the comforting familiarity of her tiny home. Then she abruptly dug her bare heels into the dirt.

"Wait. I must find my brother. I was following him when that shadow appeared."

His grip tightened, almost as if he considered physically dragging her away from danger. Then he drew in a deep breath.

"Very well, but we must be swift," he said. Without waiting for her approval, the man turned and began searching the high hedges for a sign of her missing brother. He had taken only half a dozen steps when he softly called out, "He is here."

Attempting to still the shaking that still clutched at her body, Amelia moved to stand beside her unknown savior, her gaze searching the hedge until she discovered William happily seated on the filthy ground.

Her brief flare of relief was swiftly replaced by a bout of annoyance. As always, her brother was utterly indifferent to the world, and dangers, about him.

"William, what in heaven's name are you doing?" she demanded in sharp tones.

Glancing upward, her brother offered her that sweet, heart-melting smile that never failed to touch her.

"Cats," he said, pointing at his lap.

Amelia prayed for patience as she noted the numerous kittens that had crawled into a tight ball upon his legs, along with his own stray. Well, she at least now knew where that demon-spawned cat of William's had been disappearing to at night. And precisely what he had been doing during his midnight excursions.

"Cats," William repeated with a wide smile.

"Yes, I see."

"Cats and cats."

"Yes, there are many cats, William, but it is very late. You should be in your bed. A bed you should never have left, as you well know."

William simply smiled, but at her side the shadowed gentleman stirred with growing impatience.

"We must be away from here," he said in low tones. "There is still danger."

She was not about to argue. Not when she fully agreed with his impeccable logic. She did not yet know enough of this shadow creature to be certain that it might not suddenly decide to reappear.

"Come along, William. It is time we return home."

William heaved a sad sigh, but thankfully began to replace the kittens in the hedge before clutching his renegade black cat in his arms and rising to his feet.

"Cats."

"Yes, yes. We shall visit them later."

Taking her brother's hand, Amelia joined the impatient gentleman as he turned back down the alley. In silence the three moved down the cramped lane, their footsteps echoing eerily. For a time, Amelia was simply relieved to be moving away from the nightmare that had haunted the abandoned stables. But as they continued onward, she discovered her gaze covertly studying the large male form at her side.

"Will you tell me of that creature?" she demanded in tones soft enough not to attract her brother's wandering attention.

"Perhaps. But not tonight. For now we must concentrate on returning you safely home."

She grimaced. She had expected no less. He appeared decidedly reluctant to reveal what he knew of the evil shadow.

"Then at least give me your name so I can properly thank you for rescuing me," she persisted.

"No thanks are necessary. I but did my duty."

Amelia frowned at the odd choice of words. "Duty? Surely it is not your duty to roam the darkness and rescue maidens in danger?"

Rather than answering her question, the man raised a sudden hand, bringing all three of them to a halt.

"Hold a moment."

"What is it?" she demanded in sudden fear. Dear heavens, she was not prepared for another encounter with unnatural spirits.

"Someone approaches," he answered, pointing toward the unmistakable glow of a lantern.

Peering through the darkness, Amelia breathed a sigh of relief. "Oh. It is the Watch."

"We must not be seen," the man at her side commanded in low tones.

She stiffened in surprise. "Why? We should tell them of the shadow." She gave a shiver as she recalled the recent encounter. "And there was a body on the ground . . . I think that creature murdered some poor soul."

He moved closer, the rich scent of his warm skin a welcome exchange from the stench of the alley.

"Someone was murdered, indeed. Do you wish to be the one who claims that it was a mere shadow?"

"But we both saw it. . ."

"It would not matter if the entire neighborhood witnessed the murder," he insisted, his head deliberately turning toward the silent William, who stood behind them. "The Watch cannot arrest and hang a shadow. They will desire a more tangible suspect to haul before the magistrate."

Amelia's breath caught at his horrid implication. "You cannot mean William? He has done nothing."

"Are you so certain that the authorities will believe in his innocence?"

She itched to reach up and slap him for even daring to imply someone could possibly think so ill of William. He was sweet and kind and utterly incapable of harming another soul. But even as the fury raced through her, a sensible voice urged her to consider the danger.

It was true that William was completely without guile. And that he would never lift a hand toward another. But she could not entirely deny that there were always those willing to believe the worst of her brother.

Because of his simple nature and large size, it was easy to presume that he could pose a danger. Few would take the time to discover his soft heart beneath his odd demeanor.

She gnawed her lower lip as she watched the lantern come ever closer. "Perhaps you are right."

"Follow me," he urged, stepping out of the alley and into the garden of one of the town houses.

Regaining her brother's hand, Amelia hurriedly set out after the swiftly moving form. In martyred silence, she ignored the brambles and stones that cut into her feet, and even the realization that they were blatantly trespassing from one garden to another. But as he actually angled up a path to one of the darkened houses and pulled open the kitchen door, she came to an uncertain halt.

"What are you doing?" she demanded in breathless tones.

"Leading you into my house," he retorted before he disappeared into the darkness within.

Feeling rather foolish, Amelia tugged her brother forward and stepped over the threshold. Once inside, however, she was forced to come to a halt as the darkness shrouded about her.

"A moment," the disembodied voice of her rescuer whispered through the air, sending an odd chill down her spine.

Not fear, she rather inanely realized. Instead, a stirring fascination with this man who had appeared from the darkness to save her.

There was a faint rasp of a flint before soft candlelight bathed the room.

Amelia blinked as her eyes adjusted to the sudden light. A moment later her breath tangled in her throat as she regarded the stranger.

Good heavens. He was . . . beautiful.

Fiercely, hauntingly beautiful, from his long, lustrous bronze hair that flowed past his broad shoulders to the powerful thrust of his legs. Even his unadorned black coat and breeches only served to reveal the fluid elegance of his body. Bemused, her gaze slowly lifted, tracing the crisply tied cravat to at last reach the lean countenance.

In the candlelight his features were shadowed, but there was no mistaking the startling perfection of his smooth, alabaster skin and finely sculpted features. Almost absently, she noticed that his nose was long and slender, his lips surprisingly full, and his brows the same shade as the bronze hair.

But in the end, it was his eyes that captured and held her attention.

Never had she seen eyes that were such a pure, molten silver. Eyes that glowed with a fierce intelligence. Eyes that seemed to hold her with a force she could feel to her very soul.

She should say something, a dry voice whispered in the back of her mind. Something that would bring an end to the thick, prickling silence that sent a rash of excitement over her skin.

"Oh," was all she could manage.

Thankfully unaware of her predicament, the gentleman lifted an elegant hand to wave it toward the nearby stairs.

"If you take these stairs, they will lead you to the front of the house. You may leave through the main door. Take care not to be seen."

Leave? Alone?

Amelia struggled to clear her foggy wits. "But, what of you?"

The pale countenance was grim as he glanced toward the open door. "I will ensure that the danger does not attempt to follow you. And also distract the Watch if need be."

"But . . ."

He stepped forward, those silver eyes glowing with a determined light. "See to your brother. No one must suspect that he was out of his home on this night. That is all that need concern you for now."

Her mouth opened to argue. She was unaccustomed to taking orders from anyone. Even those gentlemen who had saved her life. But before she could utter even a word, he was moving with that uncanny swiftness to press the candle into her hand and had disappeared through the open door.

She drew in a shaky breath.

Well. So far, it had been quite an evening.

She had lost her brother. Been confronted by a monstrous shadow that had ruthlessly murdered some poor soul. Been saved by a stranger. Run from the Watch. And now was abandoned in a strange house.

Oh, yes. Quite an evening.

Two

Early the next morning, Sebastian St. Ives sat alone in his library. A heavy, leather-bound book lay open upon his lap, but his attention refused to remain focused upon the ancient teachings of Plato. Instead, his pale, slender fingers tapped upon the leather chair and his narrowed gaze was trained upon the empty grate.

In the distance he could detect the faint scent of Drake. It was a scent that at the moment he barely noted. The vampire would not soon be leaving his lair. After slaying and feasting upon the blood of humans he was now cursed with the sun bane. It would not be until darkness once again claimed London that he would return to the streets.

There was another scent, however, that was far more distracting.

The scent of Miss Hadwell.

A scent that was growing ever closer.

Sebastian frowned. It was odd how easily he was able to sense the maiden. He had made a deliberate decision when he left the Veil to remain in the shadows. He was settled in a position to keep a careful eye upon the treacherous vampire—and ensure that he could halt any attempt to lure the maiden into handing over the Medallion. He was certain that in time Drake would weary of his futile games and return to the Veil.

A reasonable plan and one that had worked quite well until last evening.

His frown deepened. Last evening had changed everything.

The sight of Miss Hadwell standing in the dark as Drake crept ever closer made him realize how swiftly the vampire could strike. Had he not been on the trail of Drake, he might never have arrived before the maiden had been lured into handing over the amulet.

Even worse, upon meeting Miss Hadwell, he was forced to realize that she was not the timid, reclusive soul that he had hoped. This was no maiden who would run screaming in terror at the first hint of danger. Instead, she was bold and reckless, with a fierce determination to protect her brother. Traits that Drake would no doubt use to his full advantage.

Once again that sense of Miss Hadwell tingled through his body. She was closer. Close enough that the vision of her slender form and vivid black eyes rose easily to mind.

Too easily.

Sebastian shook his head impatiently. He was a vampire who had been pleased to turn his back on earthly passions once he'd entered the Veil. An aesthetic life devoted to acquiring knowledge and appreciating the beauty of the ancient vampire culture suited him to perfection. What could be more fulfilling than tending to one's soul?

But for all his vaulted notions, he could not deny a stark, utterly unexpected reaction to the warm, vibrant beauty of Miss Hadwell.

The passions and desires that had been all but forgotten over the centuries had tingled to sudden life. He had been unnervingly aware of the scent of her skin and the satin softness of her ripe lips. And perhaps, above all, the delicate form that had brushed against him with an innocent provocation.

Such sensations were as unwelcome as they were unexpected. Especially with the realization that he could no longer remain in the shadows as Drake stalked the young maiden. He would have to somehow ensure that he was allowed to remain close to her side.

Ruefully wishing that he were back in the Veil with nothing to occupy his thoughts but the companionship of his brethren, Sebastian slowly rose to his feet. He had put off the inevitable long enough. Miss Hadwell was close by and alone. Even if Drake was trapped in his lair, it was his duty to be at her side. There were dark companions of the vampire that could still offer danger.

As silent as smoke, Sebastian moved through his quiet home and down to the kitchen door. Once in the bright summer sunlight, he paused to allow his eyes to adjust and then used the scent of Miss Hadwell to guide his feet across the garden and down the narrow alley.

He found her by the derelict stables, her gaze carefully trained upon the ground as if searching for a lost object.

Just for a moment, his gaze lingered upon her delicate form, shown to advantage in a blue muslin gown, and the shimmering raven curls piled atop her head. She appeared so tiny, so utterly vulnerable, that his heart gave an odd lurch.

Almost as if sensing his presence, Miss Hadwell slowly turned. The dark eyes widened as he stepped forward.

"Oh." Her hand lifted to press to her heart. "You startled me."

Sebastian offered a faint bow. "Forgive me, that was not my intent." He glanced about the decrepit stables and small yard littered with rubbish. "Have you lost your brother once again?"

The tension faded from her face as her charming dimples suddenly flashed. Sebastian felt an odd warmth flow through his blood, as if the sun had abruptly emerged from behind heavy clouds.

"No, William is safely at home enjoying his breakfast."

"Ah, that is a relief." Ruthlessly shaking off the strange desire to sweep the petite maiden into his arms and carry her off to the protection of his home, Sebastian took a step forward. He had to somehow convince this overly bold woman that she could not be so recklessly indifferent to her own safety. "The streets of London can be a perilous place. Most especially when the night cloaks them in shadow."

"So I have discovered." Her smile faded and for the first time Sebastian noted the weary smudges beneath the dark eyes. "Unfortunately, William has no understanding of danger. He believes that all possess his own gentle heart."

A flare of impatience raced through him. "A grievous error and one that might lead to your own harm."

His tone was sharper than he had intended, and her expression swiftly settled into lines of defensive stubbornness.

"I have spoken with him. There is little else I can do."

Realizing his mistake, Sebastian forced back the words trembling upon his lips. For the moment it was important that he not alienate this woman. He would have to consider what was to be done with her troublesome brother at a later time.

"If it is not your brother that you seek, then what brings you to such a melancholy place?"

Her gaze slowly turned toward the shadows of the

stables, her arms wrapping about her waist in an unconscious motion.

"I could not sleep," she said slowly. "I wished . . ."

"What?"

There was a moment's pause before she grimaced.
"I wished to assure myself that I had been mistaken."

"Mistaken in what?" he asked softly.

A visible shudder raced through her. "There is no
such thing as a shadow that speaks and murders inno-
cents. It must have been fear that made me believe in
such an absurd fancy. It could not have been real."

Sebastian frowned at her troubled tones. Surely
any other maiden who had received such a fright
would wisely lock herself in her home and not return to the very spot where the demon had lurked?
Reckless, indeed.

"And so you came in search of this killer?"

"Of course not." She regarded him with a hint of
surprise. "I merely desired proof that it was a human
monster and not a figment of my nightmares."

"Ah. Have you satisfied your fears?"

She grimaced again. "Not really. There is nothing
to verify what I witnessed last evening." There was a
pause as she studied his deliberately unreadable expression. "Unless you possess an explanation?"

He did, of course. He possessed all the answers
she clearly desired. But he feared that she was not
yet prepared for the truth. Should he tell her of Drake
and the Medallion, she might very well think him
mad, or worse.

Besides which, the knowledge that a desperate
vampire was stalking her was hardly a reassuring revelation, he acknowledged ruefully. For now it seemed
preferable to worry over nightmares.

He gave a lift of his shoulder. "As I said last evening,
it is a creature of the night."

Her lips thinned at his cautious words. "That is no answer."

Sebastian stepped closer. Close enough to smell the heady scent of her warm skin.

"And will giving it a name make it any less dangerous?" he asked in low tones. "Will your fear be abandoned and your heart lightened? Man or beast, it is a thing to be avoided."

Not surprisingly, she appeared far from satisfied by his vague response. "I think you know more than you are willing to admit."

"Perhaps."

She studied him in exasperation before at last heaving a sigh. It was obvious that she sensed his adamant refusal to reveal anything more.

"Who are you?" she demanded.

His lips twitched at her unmistakable annoyance. She was not a maiden often thwarted. It did not suit her to be anything but in command of every situation.

"Such a fascination with names," he murmured.

Her nose tilted upward at his teasing, but he did not miss the sudden glint of humor in the dark eyes.

"It is only proper manners to offer an introduction. We have now spoken on two separate occasions."

"Ah well, naturally I must bow to the pressures of proper manners." Before she could guess his intention, he had reached out to grasp her hand and lifted her bare fingers to his lips. Her skin was soft as satin beneath his touch, and Sebastian found his mouth lingering as he breathed deeply of her feminine fragrance. Strange that he had forgotten the sheer pleasure of touching a young woman, he thought inanely. Or perhaps it was simply this young woman who awoke his long-buried passions. His blood stirred even as he forced himself to loosen his grip and take a step back. There was danger in such sensations. "I am Mr. Sebastian St. Ives. And you are?"

"Miss Hadwell," she retorted absently, her gaze straying to her fingers before lifting her gaze with a faint blush.

He refused to consider her flustered reaction to his touch. He was a scholar, he staunchly reminded himself. And for the moment, a reluctant guardian of this maiden.

"A pleasure, Miss Hadwell."

"You . . ." She paused to suck in a deep breath. "You are not from London?"

"No. Indeed, I have only recently arrived." He paused to glance about the rubbish that was happily rotting beneath the morning sunlight. "I am still attempting to settle among the noise and fragrant aromas of the city."

She wrinkled her nose in ready empathy. "You have not had a very pleasant welcome. I can assure you that the days are not as a rule so wretchedly hot, nor the nights so filled with such violence."

"And the noise and aromas?"

"Those, I fear, are our constant companions," she confessed, those dimples once again making an appearance.

"A pity." Arrested by the sparkle in the glorious eyes, Sebastian slowly smiled. "Still, I suppose London does have its share of beauty. Beauty that is all the more rare and astonishing because it is unexpected."

She blinked, almost as surprised as Sebastian himself at the soft words.

"Yes . . . well, I suppose there is nothing to be found here. I should return to William."

Sebastian was swift to hold out his arm. He did not want this woman to be wandering through London on her own. Not with Drake and his minions only a few houses away.

"Allow me to escort you."

She lifted her brows, as if caught off guard by his offer. "That is not necessary. I live but a short distance away."

"Not necessary, but perhaps wise." He deliberately glanced toward the ground where the traces of blood still remained. Not even this maiden could so easily have forgotten a woman had been murdered in this spot only a few hours ago. "A young maiden upon her own in such an isolated area can be prey to all sorts of undesirable attention."

With a tiny shiver she readily placed her fingers upon his arm. It appeared that her stubbornness was at least tempered with a measure of common sense.

"Very well."

Relieved that he was not to be forced into a ridiculous argument, Sebastian steered her away from the stables and down the narrow lane. He even managed to pull her close enough to feel her sweet warmth seep into his being.

For a time they walked in a companionable silence, and then Sebastian glanced down to study the delicate lines of her profile.

"Do you care for your brother on your own?"

She abruptly lifted her head to meet his searching gaze. "Oh, no. I have Mrs. Benson, my housekeeper. She is very dedicated to William."

"What of your parents?" he demanded, not at all pleased with the thought of this maiden being so heavily burdened at such a young age. It was surely unnatural, even among humans.

"They . . ." Her gaze dropped abruptly. "They struggle with their sense of regret over William. It has been very difficult for them to accept the fact that he would never be as other young gentlemen."

Sebastian held no sympathy for the unknown Hadwells. Vampires respected and admired one another precisely for their differences. It was well known that it was the variety of thoughts and opinions that made for the highest form of society, and that all possessed their share of strengths and weaknesses. All except for the three traitors who had proved unworthy of respect.

"He seems a loving and gentle soul," he said.

She gave a restless lift of one shoulder. "Yes, but there can be no denying that he is slow of wit and incapable of controlling his inheritance."

"He would not be the first son who is a disappointment to his parents," Sebastian pointed out in dry tones. He had been in London long enough to witness the wretched display of debauchery by those who claimed to be of the highest blood. "The gaming hells of London are littered with worthless noblemen squandering their inheritances."

A revealing grimace crossed her pale features. "I believe that my father would prefer such a scoundrel. As it is, he feels that William is . . ."

Her words trailed away and Sebastian instinctively covered the fingers upon his arm with a comforting hand.

"An embarrassment?"

"Yes," she whispered softly.

"But not you?"

Her head rose abruptly, the dark eyes glittering. "Of course not. William may not be like other gentlemen, but that should be rejoiced in, not feared. He does not harm others, nor lie or cheat. And certainly such a sweet man should not be locked away as if he were a dangerous animal."

Sebastian narrowed his gaze at her fierce words. He

might admire her determined love for her brother, but
that did not make him indifferent to the danger that he
posed. William was a weakness that Drake would be
swift to use to his advantage.

"No, but neither should he be allowed to lead you
into reckless folly. Last night was a near thing, my
dear. Too near."

He could feel her stiffen at his side. "William does
not make a habit of slipping off in the night. Besides
which, I have spoken very sharply with him."

Sebastian arched a knowing brow. "And you believe
that he will heed your warning?"

Her eyes revealed the truth of her unease. She
clearly was no more confident than himself that
William would halt his excursions through the dark
streets of London.

"It is all I can do," she admitted reluctantly. "I will
not have him locked in his rooms nor tied to his bed."

"So instead you will allow yourself to be put at risk?"

"If I must."

That stubborn expression had returned to her countenance and Sebastian heaved an inward sigh. He was
once again in danger of pushing her away.

"Then I hope you will call upon me if you are ever
in any need," he said gently. "I should be happy to
lend my assistance."

Without warning, she came to a halt and turned to
face him. "Why?"

He gave a blink of surprise at her sudden question.
"I beg your pardon?"

"You offer your assistance to a mere stranger. I
wonder why you would do such a thing."

"You are a young maiden on her own."

The hint of wary suspicion remained simmering
deep in the ebony eyes. "There are any number of
young maidens on their own in London, most without

the security of a home and regular allowance. Why choose me?"

Sebastian paused before deliberately curving his lips into a small smile. "Do you seek compliments, my dear? Do you wish me to tell you that I thought of you long into the night? And that I was anxious for an opportunity to speak with you again?"

Just for a moment, her breath seemed to catch at his flattering words. There was even a hint of color upon her cheeks. Then her shoulders squared sternly and she angled her chin to a stubborn tilt.

"I do not believe you."

Sebastian gave a choked laugh. "No?"

"I am not entirely ignorant. You are not a gentleman who indulges in light flirtations."

He grimaced at the truth in her accusation. Unlike Gideon and Lucien, who had joined him to battle the traitorous vampires, he had never found pleasure in pursuing mortal females. Even before the Veil, he had held himself aloof.

"No, I fear I do not possess the skill for such adventures," he confessed, his gaze lingering upon the tempting curve of her lip. "That does not mean, however, that I do not find you fascinating."

Her lips thinned in disbelief. "Perhaps as a scientist finds a bit of mold fascinating."

This time his laugh echoed through the empty lane. She was certainly a maiden who preferred to speak what was on her mind. She was also far too perceptive.

"I would hardly compare you to mold, my dear. You are far too beautiful and intelligent. A rare combination."

She waved aside his words of flattery. "What is it that you want from me, sir?"

Sebastian stepped closer, realizing that his attempts to distract her with sweet words would not satisfy her suspicion. She did not desire to wrap her world in a rosy glow that dimmed any unpleasantness, as many young maidens preferred. She would face it with a bold, fearless manner.

"For the moment I only ask for your trust," he said slowly.

The dark eyes narrowed. "Why?"

His hand was reaching out to move softly over her raven curls before he could halt the movement.

"Because I fear that danger is stalking the streets of London," he murmured. "And you are alone."

She searched his countenance, as if seeking answers. Or perhaps she was simply attempting to determine if he were friend or foe.

At last she gave a slow shake of her head.

"But you will not tell me why I am in danger? Nor why you are willing to protect me?"

"You would not believe me if I did tell you the truth."

Annoyance tightened her features as she heaved a deep sigh. She raised slender fingers to press to her temple as if to still a sudden pain.

"I weary of these riddles," she said in dark tones.

Sebastian allowed his hand to briefly cup her pale face before he ruefully stepped backward. She did, indeed, appear tired and far too fragile. His heart gave a squeeze of sympathy.

"You are very pale," he said gently. "We will speak of this again later."

"Yes, perhaps that would be for the best," she readily agreed. "Good day, sir."

He dipped his head. "Good day."

Resisting the ridiculous urge to reach out and keep her from leaving his side, Sebastian watched in silence as she slowly made her way the short distance down the alley and turned into the corner of her garden. Even from a distance he could feel the lingering anxiety that he had been unable to appease. He could feel it as sharply as if it were a part of himself.

A part of him desired to follow and wrap her in his arms so he could assure her that nothing would happen to her as long as he was near. Another part, however, urged him to return to his home and attempt to regain a measure of detachment. Nothing could be served by allowing his suddenly awakened emotions to cloud his wits.

Waiting until he was certain she was safely inside her house, Sebastian slowly turned to make his way back down the lane. He had a great deal to consider. Not the least of which was how he intended to put an end to Drake's threat.

Lost in thought, Sebastian had just passed the abandoned stables when he came to a sudden halt. Although there was nothing to be heard or seen, his senses alerted him that he was no longer alone.

With a fluid stealth, he had slipped his hand beneath his coat to grasp the hilt of his deadly dagger. Only then did he step forward to confront the lurking intruder.

"Who goes there?" he demanded in low tones. "Reveal yourself."

There was a sudden rustle among the leaves of a nearby hedge before a large, awkward form abruptly lumbered into the lane clutching a black cat.

"Me. Me."

Sebastian's tension eased as he replaced the dagger back into his hidden pocket. His expression, however, remained hard with annoyance.

"William." His brows drew together in a threatening motion. "What the devil are you doing here?"

Obviously impervious to Sebastian's dark temper, the young gentleman smiled with a sweet happiness.

"Nice man."

Sebastian's frown only deepened. "You do know that your sister believes you to be safely eating breakfast? She will be sick with worry when she discovers that you are missing once again."

William merely pointed toward the hedge. "Cats."

"Yes, I know about your damnable cats," he growled. Although he possessed compassion for the young man, the knowledge that he was so willing to lure his sister into danger was enough to set his teeth on edge. He did not doubt for a moment that Miss Hadwell would soon be scouring the streets in search of her missing brother. "What am I to do with you?"

"Me?" William wrinkled his brow. "Me, William."

"You should be at home. Did you not promise your sister to remain there?"

A familiar stubborn expression settled on the round face. "Cats."

"Blessed Nefri." Sebastian sucked in a deep breath. With an effort he calmed his rising temper. This man was a child at heart. He could not bully nor threaten him. All he could do was attempt to prevent him from leading his sister into disaster. "You are obviously determined to be with those mangy kittens regardless of the danger to your sister."

His smile returned. "Milly, nice."

"Milly?" Sebastian was briefly caught off guard. "Ah, Amelia. Yes, she is nice. Far too nice."

"Nice man."

"You are wide of the mark there, my boy," Sebastian retorted in dry tones.

William frowned. "No. Nice man."

"Blast it all." Giving a shake of his head, Sebastian surrendered to the inevitable. William was determined to be with his cats. There was only one certain means of ensuring that Miss Hadwell was not spending her nights in the dark and dangerous alley. "Get your blasted kittens."

"Cats?"

"Yes. We will take them to my home. At least then you will not be roaming the lanes and your sister will not be placed in such danger."

The frown disappeared as if by magic and the dark eyes abruptly glowed with pleasure.

"Nice, nice man," William chattered, hurriedly turning to pile the kittens in his large arms.

Sebastian suppressed a shiver. His aging housekeeper would no doubt desire his head upon a platter when she discovered his latest houseguests, if she did not simply walk out. And his privacy would be in constant danger with William wandering in and out of his home.

Still, he would do whatever was necessary to keep Miss Hadwell from Drake's clutches.

No, he sternly reminded himself. Not Miss Hadwell, but the Medallion. It was the Medallion that was important.

He heaved a heavy sigh.

"No, not a nice man," he muttered. "Merely a man who wishes he was back among the peace of his books. Now bring your cats along before I come to my senses."

Three

Amelia endured yet another sleepless night.

On this occasion, it was not the formless shadow nor the impending sense of danger that kept her pacing the floor of her bedchamber. At least not directly.

Instead it had been the memories of Mr. St. Ives that had haunted her thoughts.

Why did he disturb her so?

He was beautiful, of course. Perhaps the most beautiful man she had ever encountered. More than once she had discovered her gaze lingering upon his pale, elegant features as if she were a moonstruck idiot rather than a sensible woman.

And when he had touched her . . . well, she could not deny that he had made her heart trip and caused the most peculiar sensations to rush through her body.

But it was more than his physical appeal that made him linger in her thoughts.

There was something about him that was unusual, she acknowledged as she slowly pulled on a muslin gown in a shade of pale lemon. Something that she could not precisely pinpoint but nevertheless warned her that he was no common flirt who pursued her for his own pleasure.

The question now, of course, was—what did he want?

And how was he connected with the deadly shadow? A shadow that still remained an unnerving mystery.

Without thinking, Amelia reached up to touch the amulet. The Gypsy had warned of danger. Now, Mr. St. Ives implied that she was in peril. It made no sense, but she was not willing to dismiss the notion. However absurd, she could almost feel the sense of impending doom. As if it were slowly creeping up behind her.

Amelia shivered.

Enough of this, she sternly chastised herself. She was no coward hiding in her room. If there were danger she would face it squarely.

The brave thought had barely formed in her mind when there was a sudden rap upon the door. With a faint measure of surprise, she crossed the narrow room to discover her housekeeper standing in the hall with a harried expression.

"Oh, Miss Hadwell, I did not like to trouble you at such an early hour."

"It is no trouble," she assured the elderly servant. Although a dried-up wisp of a woman with a perpetually worried expression, Mrs. Benson had proved to be utterly loyal to both William and Amelia. "Is something the matter?"

"Well, not precisely, although it cannot be good news. I mean it never is, is it?"

Amelia blinked in confusion. "What cannot be good news?"

"That man," Mrs. Benson retorted, her thin hands wringing together. "They always mean trouble. Trouble, mark my words."

"I still do not know what you speak of, Mrs. Benson. What man?"

"That Mr. Ryan."

"Ryan?" Amelia frowned, quite certain that she had

never met a Mr. Ryan. "Are you certain he has the right house?"

The tiny head bobbed up and down. "Asked for you in particular, Miss Hadwell."

"That is odd. I have never been introduced to a Mr. Ryan. What would he be doing here?"

"He be from Bow Street, miss."

Amelia felt a chill inch down her spine. Bow Street? What would such a man be doing in her home? How would he even know her name?

"I see," she forced herself to say slowly, careful to keep her unease hidden. The housekeeper was always a breath away from a fit of the vapors. Amelia did not want to get her worked into a pucker. "Did you put him in the front parlor?"

"Aye. Were you wishing me to send him upon his way?"

It was a tempting thought. Amelia did not imagine for a moment that a Bow Street runner could bring anything but bad news. And after her sleepless nights, she felt far from confident that she could deal with any potential problem.

Unfortunately, she feared that by sending him away she was only prolonging the inevitable. If the man desired to speak with her, then he would simply return. Perhaps it was best to meet with him and be done with it.

"No, thank you, Mrs. Benson. I will see him."

"And William?"

Amelia stilled in fear. "What do you mean?"

"The man be asking for William as well."

She pressed her hands to her suddenly quivering stomach. Had someone seen William in the alley the night before last? Was it possibly that they thought him a suspect? Did they . . .

Do not panic, she chastised herself sternly. She did

not even yet know what the man wanted. It might very well be nothing to do with her.

Still, it seemed wise to keep William out of the reach of the runner. Her brother could not be trusted not to reveal more than was wise.

"Has William risen yet?" she asked in strained tones.

"Yes, Miss Hadwell. He is down enjoying a nice breakfast of fresh ham and toast."

"Would you ensure that he remains in the kitchen? I do not want him troubled by this Mr. Ryan."

An expression of determination hardened the thin features. However rattled the housekeeper might be, she would prove a formidable enemy to anyone foolish enough to threaten her beloved William.

"Depend upon me, miss. I'll not let that man trouble the sweet boy."

"Thank you." Drawing in a deep breath, Amelia forced her reluctant feet to carry her through the door and down the narrow hall. The house was too small to give her much opportunity to compose her thoughts, but she did manage a calm expression when she at last pushed open the door to the sun-filled parlor and regarded the large, boyishly handsome man that swiftly rose to his feet at her entrance. "Mr. Ryan?"

"Yes." He performed a respectable bow. "Forgive me for intruding at such an awkward hour, Miss Hadwell."

"It is no bother," she lied smoothly, moving to perch upon the edge of a brocade sofa. "Will you not be seated?"

"Thank you." He resettled his bulk on a nearby chair, his expression pleasant but unreadable.

"What is it that I can do for you?"

The runner seemed to study her composed features before clearing his throat.

"I fear I have some rather distressing news."

Amelia swallowed heavily. "Indeed?"

"Yes, two nights ago a young woman was discovered murdered not far from here."

"How . . . dreadful."

"More dreadful than you know." An unmistakable flare of frustration rippled over his broad face. "She is not the first to be so brutally slain. There has been a rash of murders for the past month. Most of the victims have been unfortunate prostitutes, but not all. There has been at least one nobleman discovered floating in the river and several less notable men who have simply disappeared."

Amelia's queasiness returned as she recalled the lifeless body that she had seen. It was a horrid image she was certain would haunt her for nights to come.

"Yes, the papers have been filled with the distressing news," she managed to murmur in low tones.

His lips twisted. "And, of course, the utter failure of the authorities to capture the madman. It has not been a pleasant summer for Bow Street."

"I suppose it has not."

With an effort, the runner forced aside his simmering irritation and managed a tight smile.

"Still, I did not come here to bemoan our lack of success. As I said, last evening there was a murder not far from here."

Amelia clenched her hands in her lap. "Do you know who she was?"

"A poor woman of the streets, I fear. She came from the stews."

"I see. It is odd that she would be in this neighborhood."

The pale eyes slowly narrowed. "We presume she was lured here rather than being forced. There was no sign of a struggle."

Amelia did not have to fake her shudder. "Poor maiden."

"Yes." There was a faint pause. "It was quite a brutal attack. For once, however, there was a witness who is willing to speak."

Amelia blinked in genuine shock. "A . . . witness?"

The runner leaned forward. "A gentleman in the neighborhood happened to be on his way home when he noticed figures moving in the alley where the body was discovered. He claimed that one was a woman and the other was a large man with dark hair."

A man with dark hair . . . it had to be William. But how? Surely they would have noticed this mysterious gentleman if he had been close enough to catch sight of William and herself? Unless . . .

Just for a wild moment Amelia considered the possibility of Mr. St. Ives whispering the horrid words into the runner's ear. Perhaps he feared that he would be implicated in the crime and had sought to distract attention. Then, just as swiftly, she was dismissing the ridiculous notion.

It had been Mr. St. Ives who had the good sense to hide William when the Watch had arrived. And had even risked returning to the dark to ensure that she could slip her brother home so no one would ever suspect he had been out of his home.

No. It could not have been Mr. St. Ives.

But, who?

"Miss Hadwell?" Mr. Ryan at last prompted her out of her tangled thoughts.

With an effort Amelia forced herself to concentrate on the man seated across the room. Despite his air of boyish good humor, she very much feared he possessed a shrewd mind and tenacious spirit. He was determined to find someone to blame for the murder.

If she were not on her guard, that someone might very well end up being William.

"I fear that I can be of no assistance, Mr. Ryan," she managed at last in reasonably steady tones. "I rarely go out in the evenings. I did not notice anything."

"A pity," he murmured. "And your brother?"

"My . . . brother?"

"I am told you have a younger brother by the name of William."

She would not flinch, she told herself sternly. She would not reveal so much as a grimace. William's very freedom might depend upon the next few moments. She must be strong.

"Yes, I do, but he would know nothing of the murder."

The pale eyes slowly narrowed at her firm words. "Perhaps it would be best if I speak with him myself."

Amelia's thin smile remained staunchly in place. "I fear that is impossible."

"Oh?" Mr. Ryan lifted his brows. "And why is that?"

"He is suffering from a fever. He has rarely left his bed for the past few days."

The runner paused as if well aware that she lied. Amelia held her breath as she waited in dread for him to demand a meeting with her brother. She did not know enough of the law to be certain she could keep him from forcing his way through her home. Then, much to her relief, he allowed a wry smile to touch his lips.

"I hope it is nothing serious?"

"No, I do not believe so," she babbled. "Still, he is very weak."

"Ah, well, then I will not trouble him," the runner said, rising to his feet.

Amelia stood and crossed toward the door. The sooner this man was out of her home, the better.

"That would be for the best, I believe."

Moving across the room, Mr. Ryan paused as he stepped through the door. "Thank you for your help, Miss Hadwell. Oh, and please tell your brother that I will return in a day or so to speak with him."

The hope that she had managed to put this man off died a swift and painful death. He would return. And on the next occasion he would insist on speaking with William.

Not even her fierce determination could keep her smile from fading to a grimace.

"I . . . very well."

"Do not bother to see me out. I can find my way."

With a bow, the large man had moved into the hall and was walking briskly toward the door. Amelia watched his retreat in troubled silence.

What was she to do?

Take William and flee?

But to where?

She could not return to her parents. As much as she loved them, she knew that the presence of William was too painful for them to bear. Within weeks they would once again be threatening to have him sent to Bedlam. And while she had her allowance, she had spent most of her savings upon this house. She could not afford to remain in hiding forever.

Besides which, a more sensible part of her warned that taking William and leaving would only make the runner more convinced of his guilt. If they did discover them they might very well have him hauled off and convicted before she could prove his innocence.

Restless and in need of a means of clearing her thoughts, Amelia found herself absently moving down the hall. She would go for a short walk, she told herself. Perhaps the fresh air and exercise would allow her to rid herself of the brooding sense of danger that continued to haunt her.

Amelia shivered as she tiptoed her way up the long staircase and slipped into the empty front salon. It was not only the heavy silence that made her cringe. Nor the squeak of worn floorboards that seemed to echo eerily through the heavy air. It was more the prickling sense of self-reproach that grew more pronounced with every step.

She should not be here, a stern voice chastised in the back of her mind. She had left her house to take a simple walk. To clear her mind and consider what was to be done. But even as she had left her home she had discovered her feet determinedly heading in a straight line to this town house. Almost as if she were being inwardly compelled to seek out Mr. St. Ives.

That compulsion had remained even when she had discovered no response to her numerous pulls upon the bell. Sensibly, she knew that she should return home. She should not even have come. But, then, she had not followed the sensible course.

Instead, before she was even aware of what she was doing, she had pushed the door open and boldly stepped into the foyer. The empty silence that greeted her only prodded her onward. The gentleman had proved to be decidedly reluctant to answer her questions, she remembered, attempting to justify her unreasonable behavior. And she was quite certain that he knew more of this shadow, and the ghastly murder, than he was willing to confess. Why should she not use this obvious opportunity to her advantage?

Glancing about the large salon, she studied the

furniture, still shrouded in covers, and the windows that did not appear to have been washed in the past several years. Amelia frowned. There was a barren, neglected air about the room. Definitely a bachelor's home, she acknowledged. Any woman would have had the house scrubbed from top to bottom before ever setting foot inside.

Indeed, it was almost as if no one lived here at all.

Gnawing upon her lower lip, she moved through the shadows, seeking some sign of occupancy. It was the right house, was it not? She could not be mistaken. This had to be the house the stranger had led her into.

Absently turning, with the vague thought of continuing her search to another room, Amelia came to a sharp halt. She had heard not a sound, but leaning negligently in the doorway was a large male form. A magnificent male form attired in a smoke gray coat and black breeches.

Oh . . . blast, she cursed silently. She was in the soup now.

A decidedly embarrassing soup.

The brilliant silver gaze was hooded as it silently flicked over her.

"So, it was not a mouse that I heard scurrying about my house, after all. Instead it is a rather unexpected guest," he murmured in his dark, honey-accented tones.

Her hand pressed her pounding heart. "Oh, Mr. St. Ives."

A bronzed brow slowly arched. "I did not expect to encounter you again so soon, Miss Hadwell. A delightful surprise, of course, but I am rather displeased with my housekeeper. She did not bother to tell me that you had arrived."

Amelia shifted uneasily. There was no ready lie to explain her wicked behavior. She had boldly been nosing about his house, like the lowest sort of sneak thief, and had been caught.

There was little to do but own up to the truth.

"No, it was not your housekeeper's fault. I did knock but there was no answer. I . . . I sneaked in so I could look about."

"Ah." The silver gaze slowly trailed down to the hands that were tightly clenched at her side. "A rather odd habit."

"It is not my customary habit," she retorted in wry tones. "As a rule, I possess all the usual manners. I suppose my only excuse is the fact that I desired to learn more of you."

Surprisingly, the full, sensuous lips twitched at her ridiculous words.

"Learn more of me? Why?"

"Well, you seem rather determined to remain a mystery. I suppose I thought to discover more of you."

He glanced pointedly about the barren room. "Among the dust sheets?"

The heat returned to her cheeks. "I realize that I was being absurd. In truth, I do not know what I sought. I am not thinking very clearly this day."

There was a moment of silence as he studied her tense countenance more closely. A sudden frown tugged at his brows.

"You are troubled? Has something occurred?"

Amelia hesitated a mere heartbeat before giving a slow nod. Perhaps it was not entirely fair to unburden her troubles upon a gentleman who was little more than a stranger. But, the need to confess her latest troubles with someone, anyone, was undeniable.

"Yes, a Mr. Ryan from Bow Street called upon me this morning. He was asking . . . questions."

The pale features hardened at her words, and for a moment Amelia was sharply reminded of the

faintly alien quality about him. It was in the elegant
perfection of his countenance and the sinuous grace
of his movements. He seemed somehow . . . above
other gentlemen. As if there were more to him than
the usual London dandies.

Thankfully unaware of her absurd thoughts, Mr. St.
Ives held out his arm.

"We must speak of this, but not here. We will be
more comfortable in the library."

Amelia found herself placing her hand upon his
arm and allowing herself to be led from the room.
Deep within her, she realized that it was certainly not
proper to be alone with this man. A maiden never
called upon a bachelor. Most especially when there
did not even seem to be a servant about.

But neither did they sneak into homes or lie to Bow
Street runners, she acknowledged wryly. It was rather
too late to become missish at this point.

In silence they moved down the shadowed hall, and
then with great care Mr. St. Ives turned her into a
large, surprisingly cheerful library.

Consuming two floors, it possessed a lovely bay
window and, far above on the ceiling, a fine rendering
of Apollo pursuing Diana.

With a hint of bemusement, she regarded the tow-
ering shelves that were bulging with an enormous
collection of leather bound books. There were hundreds, perhaps thousands. It seemed impossible to
believe that any one man could ever work his way
through such a vast number of tomes in an entire life-
time of study.

There was nothing neglected about this room, she
acknowledged as she was settled onto one of the wide
wing chairs. Everything was polished and gleamed
with loving care. It was obvious Mr. St. Ives cared

more for the privacy of his books than the more public rooms that remained shrouded in dust.

"Here you are."

With a blink, Amelia realized that her host was pressing a glass of amber liquid into her hand. She slowly lifted her gaze to meet the simmering silver eyes.

"Brandy? Is it not rather early in the day?"

He gave a lift of one shoulder. "You are pale and clearly in need of something to settle your nerves. I believe brandy is the prescribed cure for such a malady."

Well, it could not hurt, Amelia acknowledged as she lifted the glass and took a cautious sip. At first the smoky flavor filled her mouth and warmed her tongue in a rather pleasant manner; then, without warning, a fire blazed down her throat and hit her empty stomach with unexpected force.

"Ugh." With a grimace she pushed the glass back into his hand. "It is not much of a cure."

His lips twitched but he readily set aside the glass before settling upon the matching wing chair and regarding her with a steady gaze.

"Perhaps you will feel better if you tell me what the runner desired."

Folding her hands in her lap, Amelia sucked in a deep breath. "He came to me to warn that a young prostitute had been discovered murdered in the lane."

"You did not reveal that you had seen the body?" he demanded.

"Of course not." Her tongue peeked out to wet her dry lips. "But he said there had been a witness."

Mr. St. Ives abruptly stilled. "A witness? Who?"

Amelia discovered herself regarding her companion with a measure of surprise. There was an unmistakable edge of danger about him. A danger that was nearly tangible.

"Mr. Ryan said that it was a gentleman who was passing by the lane. He claimed to have seen a large man with dark hair with a woman. Then the runner asked to speak with William."

"I presume you refused?" he asked in rather distracted tones.

"Yes, I said William had been ill and in bed for the past few days."

Far from being shocked by her blatant lies, Mr. St. Ives gave an approving nod.

"That is well. I do not believe that William would comprehend a need for silence."

"No, but I do not think that Mr. Ryan was entirely convinced," she confessed with a worried frown. "I fear he is quite intent upon seeking out William to question him."

"A problem, certainly," he murmured.

Amelia's frown deepened. He appeared oddly preoccupied, as if he were barely attending to her words.

"What is it?"

His pale fingers tapped a restless tattoo on the arm of his chair. "It is odd."

"Odd?"

"This witness claims to have seen a man with dark hair and a woman?"

Amelia stifled a surge of impatience. "Yes."

"If it was your brother who the man observed, then who was the woman?" he demanded in low tones. "You did not find William until we were together. It is not possible that this witness could have seen you alone with your brother. So why did he lie?"

Four

Sebastian watched in silence as the young maiden pondered his words. It was obvious that she had been too rattled by the appearance of the runner to consider with clarity the claim of the witness. Now she ruthlessly gnawed her lower lip as her swift wits attempted to make sense of the insensible accusation.

A sharp, poignant desire to soothe her poor, maltreated lip swept through Sebastian with shocking force.

He closed his eyes briefly. Perhaps ridiculously, he had hoped that the hours he had devoted to lecturing himself upon the danger of heedless passions would have rid him of the peculiar awareness that afflicted him when this maiden was near. Or at least allowed him to keep such tempting sensations at bay.

She had only to enter his home, however, for him to realize that his lectures had been futile. For whatever unfathomable reason, this woman managed to stir to life a heat and desire that had never plagued him before.

Seemingly unaware of the prickles of awareness that skittered through his body, Miss Hadwell at last met his probing gaze with a bewildered frown.

"Perhaps the witness was mistaken. Perhaps he saw the two of us together."

Sebastian grimaced. He already possessed his own suspicions of this supposed witness. It had the stench of Drake.

"I do not have dark hair," he pointed out in low tones. "And besides, I would have known if there were another near."

She lifted her slender hands. "Then perhaps William did see the woman before we arrived. He might even have spoken with her."

His expression hardened. "I do not believe William noticed anything beyond his beloved kittens. And there is still the true murderer who must be accounted for."

A visible shudder raced through her as he forced her to realize that it had been no simple mistake that had led the runner to her door.

"But why?" she whispered in an unsteady tone. "Why would the man lie?"

"He obviously desired to have William implicated in the murder."

The dark eyes were nearly black as she struggled to accept the truth. "Who? Who would do such a ghastly thing?"

"That I intend to discover, my dear," he said grimly.

"This is horrible." Without warning, she covered her face with her hands, as if battling the urge to cry. "Poor William."

Barely aware that he was moving, Sebastian had slipped from his chair to kneel beside her. He might rue her brash spirit and reckless bravery, but he realized that he could not bear to see it broken. His heart clenched in pain as he reached out to gently place an arm about her shoulders.

"Do not fear, Amelia," he said softly. "I will let nothing happen to you."

Her eyes slowly lifted to regard him with a haunted gaze. "I do not fear for myself."

His lips twisted in a wry manner. Of course she did not fear for herself. She would bravely storm the flames of the nether world. She would march onto the battlefields of Napoleon with her head high. She would no doubt face death itself without flinching.

Her only weakness was her brother.

A weakness that the treacherous Drake had clearly decided to use to his own advantage.

"No," he agreed as his fingers absently stroked the satin skin of her shoulder. "I realize you possess no concern for yourself."

She seemed taken aback by his words. "That is not true."

"When was the last occasion you simply did something for your own pleasure?" he demanded in soft tones. "A walk in the park, reading a book, attending a party?"

"I find pleasure in seeing my brother secure and happy," she retorted defensively.

His fingers tingled as they traced aimless patterns upon her skin. "You, my dear, are a most unusual woman."

A reluctant hint of amusement glinted in the dark eyes. "Should I be insulted?"

"No, it is a most sincere compliment." He studied the delicate features, lingering a heartbeat upon the temptation of her mouth. "Although I will admit a grudging compliment."

She lifted her brows. "What do you mean?"

Sebastian knew that he should move to a less perilous position. Her distress had been controlled and the familiar unquenchable spirit was once again sparkling in her eyes. But his body refused to obey the commands of his common sense.

It was far too delightful to touch her in such an intimate manner.

"I am a gentleman who has devoted his life to the study of logic," he admitted dryly. "I am unaccustomed to being . . . distracted by young maidens."

He heard her breath catch as her eyes widened in surprise. "You find me distracting?"

"Dangerously so."

She regarded him closely, as if seeking some truth there. "Are you just saying this to try and charm me?"

Sebastian gave a low chuckle, his hand moving to cherish the delicate lines of her face.

"If I desired simply to charm you, I would tell you that your eyes possess the dark velvet beauty of a midnight sky." His fingers brushed over her mouth. "Or that your lips are so lush and full that they entice a gentleman beyond bearing."

He felt a shiver race through her. A shiver that was echoed within himself. Then she gave a breathy laugh.

"I was mistaken."

"Mistaken?"

"You are far more proficient at flirtation than I suspected," she murmured.

His lips twisted with rueful humor. "No, you were quite correct, my dear. As I said, I am a simple scholar and not at all prepared for the likes of you."

A sudden heat filled her cheeks as she gazed at him through the tangle of her long, black lashes.

"Do you mind?"

Finding it absurdly difficult to concentrate upon her words, Sebastian leaned even closer to the damnable temptation of her lips.

"Mind what?"

"Being distracted," she whispered.

"Yes." His mouth hovered a mere breath from her

own. "Unfortunately, there appears to be little I can do."

"Oh."

A heartbeat passed as Sebastian trembled on the edge of blissful madness. One move, a mere tilt of his head, and he could explore the sweetness that beckoned him.

Her lips would be warm and satin-soft with the taste of innocence. They would gently part to invite a more intimate exploration as she arched to press her curves next to his aching body.

Sharp, dazzling heat raced through his blood, stirring the dark passions that had lain dormant for so long.

Thankfully, it was that very heat that abruptly brought him back to his sadly forgotten senses.

Sucking in a sudden breath, he surged to his feet. His body felt heavy and tight with an unfamiliar need. A need that he grimly ignored. He had to halt this foolishness. He could not allow himself to be distracted. No matter what the temptation.

"Perhaps we should return our attention to the reason you sought me out," he forced himself to murmur.

For a moment it appeared that she was finding it as difficult as he was to shake off the lingering awareness of what had happened between them. There was a bemused expression and a hint of fire deep in the midnight eyes. Then, with a stifled gasp, she was on her feet.

"William! Good heavens, I nearly forgot. What am I to do?"

He absently pushed his fingers through the hair he had left loose. "For the moment, I fear there is nothing to be done."

It was clearly not at all what she wished to hear.

"But what of Mr. Ryan? He is determined to speak with my brother."

"He has nothing more than a vague description of a large gentleman with dark hair. That could easily include half the gentlemen in London."

She wrapped her arms about her tiny waist. "Yes, but not half of the gentlemen in London were in the lane during the murder," she pointed out in worried tones. "Once he speaks to William, he might very well be convinced he is guilty. If only . . ."

Her words trailed away, and Sebastian stepped forward as an odd expression crossed over her countenance. He experienced a decided chill. He already sensed that the expression could mean nothing but trouble.

"What?"

She nibbled her bottom lip as she considered her inner thoughts. "If only we knew who did commit the murder, then William would be safe."

The chill struck again and Sebastian regarded her with a guarded expression. "You intend to reveal to Mr. Ryan that you saw a shadow kill the maiden?"

"Of course not. He would think me mad. And besides, I would have to confess I was not at home with William as I told him."

"Then what do you speak of?"

Her features hardened abruptly. "I will discover the truth of this shadow myself."

Although he had expected something ridiculous and carelessly imprudent, Sebastian still found himself caught off guard.

"No."

She flinched at his sharp refusal, her spine stiffening and her chin rising in an ominous manner.

"I beg your pardon?"

Sebastian was intelligent, even for a vampire. His

mind was well honed and trained to seek the truth. He had even studied the philosophies of mortals so he could possess a greater understanding of their tumultuous existence.

The moment called for subtle manipulation, whispered the voice of reason in the back of his mind. A gentle hand upon her reins. To challenge her pride blatantly would make her more determined than ever to behave the fool.

His intelligence at the moment, however, was astonishingly absent as he regarded the stubborn female with rising annoyance. She would not be allowed to put herself, nor the Medallion, in peril. Not for any reason.

"I have warned you of the danger," he retorted in clipped tones. "The creature that attacked that woman would kill you without mercy."

The dark eyes narrowed abruptly. "How do you know? What do you hide from me?"

"This is no harmless diversion, Amelia. Thus far it has been sheer luck that your reckless nature has not brought you sorrow. Such luck will not remain forever."

Her hands landed upon her hips in open defiance. "If you will not tell me the truth, then I must discover it for myself. I will not allow anyone to harm William."

Sebastian battled the urge to reach out and shake some sense into her. "You will risk death?"

The color drained from her at his stark question but she never faltered. "If I must."

"This is foolishness," he growled. "I forbid you even to consider such an absurd scheme."

"Forbid me?" The features hardened with a dangerous determination. "By what right?"

"The right of common sense," he retorted in exasperation. "If you wish to protect your brother, then

return home and make sure he is not allowed to roam
the streets."

"I do not need your consent, Mr. St. Ives. I am in
command of my life and make my own decisions."

"Decisions fit only for a wayward child."

Even as the angry words flew from his lips, Sebastian realized his error. Nothing, nothing could have
been more perfectly calculated to make her dig in her
heels.

Visibly bristling in anger, Amelia drew in a shaky
breath. "I believe you have said quite enough, sir. I
will wish you a good day and assure you that I shall
not trouble you further."

"Amelia . . ." He stepped forward, intending to
make amends for his hasty words, but even as he held
out a hand she was whirling on her heel and storming toward the door. He could follow, of course. She
could not outrun him. She could not hide. But for the
moment, he realized it would be futile. There was no
doubt that she was being devilishly stubborn. And
more than reckless. Still, he could not lay the entire
blame upon her shoulders. She did not truly understand the danger. She could not possibly realize that
the shadow she sought was a legendary vampire that
could brutally kill her before she could blink. Until
she knew the truth, she would rush blindly into danger and risk everything for her blasted brother.
"Bloody hell."

Not surprisingly, Amelia returned home in a foul
mood.

The man was an impossible, arrogant, overbearing
beast, she told herself as she stormed to her home and
slammed the door with a force that made her teeth
rattle.

He had no right to order her about as if she were a child. For heaven's sake, she had boldly established her own life, her own household, and taken on the care of her brother. She had far more responsibilities than most females twice her age.

And she had been plodding along quite well without the interference of Mr. Sebastian St. Ives, she reassured herself grumpily.

Quite, quite well.

But as the day passed, her wounded pride had slowly given way to common sense.

Sebastian St. Ives had no right to give her orders, or even to question her decisions. He had been high-handed and utterly out of line. But despite his harsh words, she sensed that it had not been mere arrogance that had caused his annoying behavior.

Instead she sensed that his anger had come from a very genuine concern for her welfare, a concern that had been absent from her life for so long that she found it difficult to accept.

Ruefully, she began to realize that perhaps she had overreacted. She was so accustomed to battling for her right to defend and protect her brother that she had instinctively lashed out. It was now so deeply ingrained that she did not always realize when her heart was overruling her common sense.

And, too, if she were being completely honest with herself, she had to admit that a portion of her prickly reaction had been pure self-preservation.

She might not fully understand why her blood tingled and her heart raced when she was near Sebastian. Or even why he lingered in her thoughts when she had far more important matters to ponder. But she was wise enough to realize that her awareness made her wish for dangerous things. Feelings and sensations better left forgotten.

She was still pacing aimlessly when a noise from the garden had her moving toward the window. Just for a moment, her heart stopped and she feared what she might discover prowling in the dark. A shadow. A killer. A monster.

Instead, her eyes caught sight of the sleek, black cat that prowled haughtily across the garden, knocking over a crumbling statue and a forgotten bucket as he slowly strolled toward the nearby hedge.

Her momentary fear shifted to annoyance. The noise the cat was making was certain to wake William. Gads, it might wake the entire neighborhood. And when he discovered his beloved pet missing, nothing would keep him from going in search.

Blast, blast, blast.

How could she risk having her brother out of the house? Not only did she worry that the madman might return, but she could not deny a lingering fear that Mr. Ryan might be lurking about the neighborhood, hoping to capture her brother the moment he appeared.

The answer, of course, was that she could not.

With a heavy sigh, Amelia reluctantly made her way through the silent house and into the garden. Although she had boastfully stated she would do whatever necessary to protect William, she was not completely witless, no matter what Sebastian might claim. Indeed, she was quite intelligent enough to feel a measure of unease as she pursued the demon-spawned cat across the garden and around the narrow town house.

She would not go far, she promised herself silently. No further than the end of the block. After that, the stupid cat would be on its own.

Almost as if sensing her determination, the stray hovered a moment at the edge of the narrow street before streaking across the pavement to the tall hedge. From the leafy concealment, two shining eyes regarded Amelia, as if daring her to come and rescue him.

Muttering a string of curses wholly unfit for a proper young maiden, Amelia marched across the street and bent down to attempt to recover the beast. One day she would discover precisely how the cat continued to find its way from the house, and then she would bring a firm end to these midnight outings. A very firm end.

Intent upon her efforts to force her arms through the hedge and still uttering words fit only for a stable hand, Amelia took little note of the odd chill that suddenly seemed to fill the air. Not even when a rash of goose bumps feathered over her skin.

"Ah. A most peculiar, if rather delightful, sight."

Amelia nearly leaped from her skin at the sound of the faintly mocking voice. With a small squeak she abruptly straightened to discover a handsome gentleman with golden curls and elegant attire standing mere inches from her.

"Oh."

"Did I startle you? Forgive me—that certainly was not my intention."

The stranger smiled, but Amelia was unnervingly aware that it did not quite reach the hard, dark eyes. She took an instinctive step backward. Despite the aristocratic features and refined manners, there was something about this gentleman she did not trust.

"I fear that I did not hear you approach."

He deliberately lifted his brows. "You appeared quite involved with the hedge. Have you perhaps lost something of value?"

"My brother's cat," she reluctantly confessed.

"Ah. Allow me." Before Amelia could protest, the

man had reached into the hedge and, with disgustingly little effort, plucked the renegade cat through the branches. He even managed to ignore the spitting and hissing as he placed the stray into Amelia's arms. "There we are."

Attempting to calm the cat that continued to hiss in anger at the stranger, she forced a measure of gratitude to her countenance.

"You must forgive this ungrateful wretch. He is a stray who has never learned a modicum of good manners."

That cold smile widened to reveal large, white teeth. "I, on the other hand, have always possessed the most exquisite manners. Allow me to introduce myself. Mr. Ramone, at your service."

He performed a half bow and Amelia forced herself to ignore the urge to flee to the safety of her house. He had, after all, saved William's pet.

"A . . . pleasure."

Mr. Ramone regarded her with a razor-sharp gaze. "And you, of course, must be Miss Hadwell."

Amelia sucked in a sharp breath. How could this stranger possibly know her name?

"Have we met before?"

"No, but the agent pointed you out when he first showed me the town house I have rented for the season. I believe he presumed that I would view the neighborhood more favorably if I realized such a beautiful maiden was near. He was quite correct."

She clutched the cat tighter, not at all fond of the thought that this man might have been watching her when she was unaware.

There was something . . . wrong about him.

"You live near?" she forced herself to inquire.

He waved a thin, pale hand toward the house behind the hedge. "Only a few steps away."

"I see."

Almost as if sensing her odd revulsion, his thin lips twitched. "I have been seeking an opportunity for an introduction, but you have proved to be remarkably evasive."

She covertly shifted even further from the looming gentleman. If it were up to her, she would be even more evasive in the future.

"I live very quietly."

"Yes, I know." He deliberately glanced toward her darkened home. "With your brother William, is it not? A charming young gentleman."

"You know my brother?" she demanded in surprise.

"We have occasionally crossed paths." His gaze abruptly returned to her, dark eyes glittering in the moonlight. "There are, of course, those in the neighborhood who warn that he is dangerous, but I pay little heed to such nonsense."

She stiffened in outrage at his offhand words. "My brother is not dangerous."

"Certainly not." The thin fingers touched the golden curls, as if to ensure they were still in perfect order. "As I said, I find him to be quite charming. Unfortunately, there are always those who delight in believing the worst of others."

"They are fools," she said between clenched teeth.

"Perhaps." He gave a smooth shrug. "Still, I do feel it incumbent upon me to warn you that there have been a few rather unfortunate rumors."

Although she had already suspected that gossip would be flying about the neighborhood, Amelia discovered her stomach heaving with queasiness.

"What rumors?"

"That poor William was somehow involved in the death of that woman."

Her breath caught. It was all so utterly unfair, she

seethed grimly. William was the very last person who
would harm another. Those who did not truly know him
had no right to make such ghastly judgments.

"It is not true."

"I did not believe so for a moment." Mr. Ramone
pressed a hand to his heart, as if to show his sincerity,
but once again she was aware of the cold hardness of
his gaze. "Indeed, I have done my best to put a firm
halt to such unpleasant speculations."

"I . . . thank you," she forced herself to mutter.

He took a step closer, ignoring the cat, which continued to hiss at him in warning. Just for a moment,
that remorseless gaze seemed to flick down to the
amulet that hung about her neck, but it lifted so
quickly it was impossible to be certain.

"However, it does not improve matters to have a
Bow Street runner asking questions about your
brother. It encourages others to consider him guilty,
whether he is or not."

Amelia's lips thinned. Did he think she was ignorant?
Of course she realized Mr. Ryan's blatant interest in
William was bound to cause trouble. Unfortunately, she
had yet to be put in charge of Bow Street.

"There is little I can do to stop Mr. Ryan from asking questions," she retorted with a decided snap.

The carved features hardened briefly in a dangerous
fashion before he was visibly sheathing his emotions
behind a mask of seeming compassion.

A compassion that made her as uneasy as any display of anger.

"I did not mean to upset you, Miss Hadwell," he
said in oily-smooth tones. "I only speak of William's
troubles out of concern. I wish you to know that if you
ever have need, you may depend upon me."

"That is very kind, but unnecessary, I assure you."

That cruel hardness returned to his expression at her firm words. His smile, however, never faltered.

"Without modesty, I assure you that I can offer you whatever protection you need."

The chill in the air deepened abruptly and Amelia unconsciously licked her dry lips. She wanted to be away from this man, she suddenly realized. As far away as possible.

"I must return home."

The false smile disappeared abruptly. Amelia tensed, not at all certain the man would willingly allow her to simply walk away. His gaze once again strayed toward the amulet that glowed softly in the moonlight. He stiffly offered her a bow.

"Of course. It is very late." He straightened, the thin face appearing almost skeleton-like in the shadows. "You will recall my offer, I trust?"

"Yes."

Dipping a hurried curtsy, Amelia turned away, more relieved than she cared to admit at the thought of being away from Mr. Ramone. But even as she was nearing the safety of her home, Amelia suddenly halted.

There was a smell in the air. Cold steel, and something rather foul. A frown pulled at her brows. What was that odor? And why did she sense that she had smelled it before?

Oddly, it seemed vitally important that she remember.

"Is something the matter?"

Amelia jumped as she realized she was foolishly lingering in the dark street when she should be hurrying home with all speed.

"No. Good night."

Not allowing herself the opportunity to be distracted again, Amelia hurriedly crossed the street and entered the blessed familiarity of her garden.

Sebastian had been right, she admitted ruefully.

She had been a fool to roam the streets at this hour. Even if it had been to ensure the safety of William. Only sheer luck had kept her from being harmed.

A luck that was destined to fail her eventually.

Five

Sebastian knew the moment Amelia left the protection of her home. Just for a moment, he froze in disbelief; then, tossing aside the large book he had been futilely attempting to study, he swept across the library and down the stairs.

Bloody hell. He would throttle her, he silently cursed as he charged through the house and out the back door. Although she had boldly claimed she would go in search of the killer who stalked the streets, he had not thought she would be so foolish. Well, at least not foolish enough to begin any such search during the middle of the night, he swiftly amended.

Now, because of her stubborn courage, she was alone and vulnerable. He had to reach her before she could be harmed.

Then he would throttle her.

Entering the garden, Sebastian never paused as he slipped toward the dark lane. Without being fully bonded with Amelia, he could only sense that she was somewhere ahead of him, but he knew that the closer he came to her the easier it would be to locate her.

Despite his attention being sharply focused upon Amelia, Sebastian did not miss the faint prickle that raced over his skin.

Halting his steps, he carefully considered his

surroundings. There was a vampire near. Very near. And oddly able to mask his identity.

His expression hardened with determination. He did not know who the mysterious vampire was, but he was certain that it posed a danger to Amelia. He would have to deal with the threat before he could return the maiden to her home.

Cautiously angling across the lane, Sebastian allowed his senses to lead him toward the derelict stables. There was no noise, no indication that there was anyone near, but he did not hesitate. Entering the darker shadows of the stables, he stepped over a fallen beam and glanced about the empty stalls and overhead loft.

For a moment there was nothing to see. Nothing beyond dust and cobwebs. Then, just when he was beginning to wonder if he had been mistaken, a faint fog began to form in a distant corner.

More out of instinct than actual fear, Sebastian reached beneath his coat to remove the dagger. He would prefer to avoid a fight if possible. Violence was abhorrent to him, and violence toward a brother was nearly unthinkable. But, he would not allow Amelia to be harmed. Whatever it might take.

Keeping a careful watch on the fog that continued to move ever closer, Sebastian once again attempted to determine who it was that stalked ever nearer. A frown marred his brow as he sensed nothing but emptiness in the fog. It was as if it were no more than an illusion.

Which was ridiculous. He had distinctly perceived the presence of a vampire. It was here. Somewhere.

Clenching the dagger in his hand, he heard nothing but his own shallow breathing. Nothing until there was a faint scrape behind him. Attempting to turn, he was halted as a sudden, searing pain abruptly flared through his body.

With a gasp of agony, Sebastian fell to his knees. From behind, someone was relentlessly stabbing him with a sharp blade, the steel digging deep into his body and twisting before being wrenched out and thrust in again. He attempted to twist away but the blade followed. Over and over it bit into his flesh, the sheer savagery of the attack nearly overwhelming.

Through a haze, Sebastian could feel the hot, sticky flood of blood seeping over his skin, and worse, his strength was being ruthlessly drained away.

He had to do something. And soon.

Ignoring the white blaze of agony, Sebastian leaned forward until his hands touched the dirt. He was careful to keep a grip on the dagger; then, with a grim effort, he kicked his leg out behind him. His foot connected solidly with a leg and he was rewarded by the sound of a muffled grunt. He would not go quietly, he promised himself. Once again he kicked out, but with frustrating speed, his attacker managed to slip to one side.

Realizing his danger, Sebastian attempted to angle his head away from the vampire, but his movements were sluggish and a heavy object connected with his skull with rattling force. The world went momentarily dark before he forced himself back toward the pain that throbbed relentlessly. No. He had to remain conscious. If he were to be overcome, then Amelia would be helpless.

He sensed the mysterious attacker had once again lifted his arm to strike another blow and with sheer desperation he flung himself to one side. At the same moment a sound from the doorway of the stable echoed through the air.

Having sacrificed the last of his fading energy,

Sebastian could do nothing to stop the villain from attacking him, nor the intruder. Instead he could only lie upon the hard ground as he rasped agonized breaths.

Inwardly, he cursed his weakness, but he knew he could do nothing. Without rest to restore his strength he was as helpless as a babe.

Barely keeping the darkness at bay, Sebastian vaguely heard the sounds of approaching footsteps and the dry hiss of an indrawn breath. A part of him awaited the blow that would send him into oblivion; at the same time, he ludicrously clutched the dagger as if he hoped the fool would conveniently lie down next to him so he could stab him.

He supposed that time passed, although it was difficult to determine with his head filled with fog. Then, soft and comforting hands touched his face.

"Sebastian, can you hear me?" a husky female voice whispered near his ear.

He lifted his head, only to discover that his right eye had swollen shut.

"Who is it?"

"Nefri."

A sigh was wrenched from his burning throat. He was saved. The ancient vampire was by far the most powerful of all. Even without the Medallion. None would challenge her.

He did not know what had brought her to the abandoned stables, but he had never been more relieved in his Immortal life.

He coughed, the bitter taste of blood filling his mouth. "Forgive me for not rising," he said wryly.

"Be at ease, my dear." The elder vampire gave a disapproving click of her tongue as her hands ran lightly over his battered body. "Without the Medallion, I can not heal you properly."

Sebastian opened his one eye to assure her that he only needed rest when a searing heat abruptly raced through his blood. His teeth clenched in shock and his legs jerked. He felt as if he were being roasted from the inside out. Then, as swiftly as the heat had struck, it was fading.

Surprisingly, Sebastian discovered the throbbing aches had muted to a near-bearable level, and that he was even capable of rising to a sitting position. Standing, however, was still out of the question.

"That is better," he murmured. "Thank you."

"Just remain here for a bit. You must give yourself time to recover."

As the darkness receded, Sebastian began to regain a portion of his shattered wits. With Nefri near, there was little to fear. Still, he wanted to ensure that he was not about to face another savage attack.

"The vampire . . . he is gone?"

Nefri shifted so that she was kneeling within view of his undamaged eye. He was rather surprised to discover she was attired in a bright, patched skirt and the loose blouse generally associated with a Gypsy. Her silver hair hung about her shoulders and her arms were covered with numerous bracelets. It was her expression, however, that at last captured and held his attention. Even in the shadows, he could tell that it was troubled.

"Yes, he is gone."

"It was odd. I could sense his presence, but not his identity. He is very powerful."

Nefri nodded slowly. "And very dangerous. Whoever this is, he has called upon ancient powers that have been forbidden."

Sebastian swallowed a curse. His return to London was proving to be complicated enough without the added distraction of a vampire using dark powers.

"Do you know who it is?"

"No. I do fear, however, that he is determined to claim the Medallion."

Medallion. Sebastian's heart came to a frozen halt as he recalled the reason he had left his home in the first place.

"Amelia," he breathed in anxious tones.

Nefri gave a rueful nod of her head. "Yes. While you were being lured to these stables, she was confronted by Drake."

Instinctively he attempted to rise, only to fall back to his knees as a wave of dizziness rushed through him.

"Damn."

A gnarled hand reached out to touch his shoulder. "Do not fear. She is safely returned home."

He exhaled a sharp breath of relief, although his expression remained tight with concern. The woman was going to drive him to madness. To even think of her being in the company of Drake while he was incapable of rushing to her rescue was enough to make his stomach clench and the throbbing in his head increase to a nearly unbearable level.

"She is . . . difficult," he muttered in disgust.

The elder vampire lifted her brows. "She possesses the spirit necessary to protect the Medallion, I will agree."

"Oh yes, she possesses a wretched amount of spirit," he swiftly agreed, his hand reaching to touch the deep gash on his temple. "Unfortunately, she has no notion of the danger she courts so blithely."

Nefri tilted her head to one side, as if considering his words.

"I believe she senses the danger, but she is a woman who feels a very deep sense of loyalty. One cannot fault her for such a commendable trait."

Oh no? At the moment, Sebastian would willingly

do more than fault her stubborn sense of loyalty. What good would such a wondrous trait do her if she were to be killed?

"That loyalty might very well endanger the Medallion," he retorted, not at all prepared to admit that his frustration was more in fear for Amelia than the ancient artifact. "She will do whatever is necessary to keep her brother safe. Including handing her amulet to Drake if she had to."

Nefri regarded him with a steady gaze. "There is that danger, certainly."

He growled impatiently. "Then why do you leave the Medallion with her?"

A faint smile touched the lined countenance. "You must understand—the Medallion is more than mere metal. It has been imbued with blessings that allow it to bestow powers upon the one who has it. In return, however, the Medallion takes on the qualities of whoever possesses it. Goodness or evil. Love or hate. That is why I chose Miss Hadwell. For her courage and ability to care so deeply for her brother. It is also why it is so important to stop the traitors. In the wrong hands, the power of the Medallion would be terrible indeed."

Sebastian frowned. As a scholar he had, of course, studied the Medallion. He understood the history and the powers. He had even managed to unravel the complex spell that had been used to create the Veil with the assistance of the Medallion. Still, he had not truly considered the artifact's ability to echo the qualities of who might possess it.

Nefri had clearly considered the maidens she had chosen to bond with the amulets. He could hardly protest her choice simply because he was becoming far too attached to Amelia.

He heaved an unconscious sigh. "Then perhaps it should be another who is sent to protect Miss Hadwell."

The vampire blinked in surprise. "Why?"

"I have managed to do no more than prod her into foolish behavior. She does not trust me."

Her unwavering gaze regarded him for a long moment. "I believe that you underestimate yourself, Sebastian," she at last said softly. "You possess a quiet, studious nature, but your strength is undeniable. Miss Hadwell will turn to you in her time of need."

Sebastian unconsciously grimaced, recalling the harsh words that he had exchanged with Amelia only a few hours earlier.

"I fear she is more likely to believe she is capable of facing any danger on her own. She is extraordinarily fearless."

"Then we must simply do what we can to protect her, with or without her awareness," Nefri said firmly.

He paused a long moment, his heart troubled. "Yes."

Easily sensing his lingering disquiet, Nefri leaned forward to regard him with a hint of concern.

"Sebastian, is there something more troubling you?"

He briefly considered denying his most pressing hesitation. He was supposed to be a gentleman of sense. A gentleman who observed and studied others with a scholar's aloof objectivity. It was not easy to admit, even to himself, that he had somehow lost that necessary edge.

"I am not as . . . detached as I should be," he reluctantly confessed.

Surprisingly, Nefri raised her brow as if puzzled by his admission.

"And why do you believe you should be detached?"

Sebastian frowned. "If I am to outwit Drake, then

I must have my senses clear. Something that is impossible when Miss Hadwell is near."

Without warning, the vampire gave a low chuckle. "Do not fret, Sebastian. You are perfectly suited to be a Guardian for the Medallion."

Sebastian could not find the humor in his situation. Indeed, he found it all utterly frustrating.

"Oh, I have proved to be quite a Guardian," he said dryly, his fingers still pressed to the slowly healing wound upon his temple. "I cannot even protect myself."

Nefri clicked her tongue. "Do not blame yourself. The vampire you battled tonight possessed great powers. Powers perhaps even greater than my own."

Sebastian could not halt a small shiver as he recalled the fierce attack. There had been something unnerving in the cunning manner he had been lured into the stables and the savagery of the villain. There was also a lingering puzzlement as to the motive for the attack.

Had it simply been designed to allow Drake to be alone with Amelia?

Or had it been meant to put a permanent end to him? And if so, why had the vampire not finished the task? If he were willing to use forbidden powers, he could have destroyed him. Or placed him under a spell that would have held him captive for an eternity.

"But who?" he demanded in harsh tones. "And why attack me?"

Nefri's countenance hardened with a bleak expression. "Those are questions that I fear will be answered soon enough."

After yet another restless night, Amelia rose and attired herself in a muslin gown the soft shade of daffodil. She even took extra care with the raven curls that she piled atop her head, leaving a handful to softly frame her face.

A glance in the mirror assured her that only close scrutiny would reveal the shadows that darkened her eyes and the faint hint of strain upon her features. It was important that she hide her prickling sense of unease. She did not want William or Mrs. Benson fretting needlessly. Having to devote her days to comforting and reassuring them was an additional burden she did not desire.

Smothering a sigh, she ran her hands over the soft muslin of her skirt and squared her shoulders. She was already late for breakfast. If she did not show herself downstairs soon, Mrs. Benson would be in search of her. The mere thought of her squawking was enough to make her teeth clench.

With a measured step she left the peace of her chambers and made her way to the lower floor. She discovered a portion of her lingering alarm fading beneath the bright summer sunlight that tumbled through the wide windows. Mrs. Benson had even filled the rooms with freshly cut flowers that managed to mask the less pleasant aromas that drifted from the streets.

Entering the small breakfast room, she was surprised to discover that William had already eaten his meal and departed. As a rule he remained, awaiting her arrival, regardless of how late she might be.

Her brows pulled together in concern. Surely he had not left the house—not after her stern lectures.

Standing in the center of the room, Amelia more sensed than heard someone enter behind her and she swiftly turned to find her housekeeper bustling in with a tray to clear the table.

"Oh, Mrs. Benson, have you seen William?" she demanded, before she could stop the words.

Rather than responding with her usual fuss, Mrs. Benson merely smiled with a surprising satisfaction.

"Yes, he is in the front salon with his visitor."

Amelia blinked in surprise. "A visitor?"

"A Mr. St. Ives. William appeared right pleased to have him call. A nice change from moping about with his long face."

Sebastian.

Suddenly Amelia was aware of that familiar tingle that was racing through her blood. Of course. If not for her distraction, she would have already known that he was near. Perhaps a ridiculous fancy, but one she could not dismiss.

There were times when he rose to mind that she could almost believe that she could actually feel his thoughts and emotions.

Ridiculous, indeed.

"Thank you," she murmured, already moving toward the door. She needed to see Sebastian. She wanted to ensure that her hasty words of yesterday had not made him utterly despise her.

"I'll be having a nice tea tray prepared in a few moments," Mrs. Benson called after her, in a considerably happier frame of mind than she had been in some days. Amelia could only presume the poor woman had wearied of merely having William and herself as distractions. Any guest would be a blessing.

Resisting the urge to rush down the hall to the front parlor, Amelia instead kept a stately pace and managed to enter the room with every semblance of composure.

That did not mean her heart did not instinctively leap at the sight of his striking features and the bronzed hair that had been left unbound to fall against his shoulders. Or that a disturbing heat did not pool in the pit of her stomach as his silver gaze ran an appreciative gaze over her slender form. Only that she managed to hide her fierce reaction with at least a resemblance of equanimity.

The moment she stepped through the open door, Sebastian was swiftly at her side, a rather guarded expression on his face.

"Good morning, Amelia."

She smiled warmly, simply happy to have him near. "Mr. St. Ives."

"Please, I prefer Sebastian."

The behavior that her mother had drilled into her for years insisted that such intimacy was improper, but Amelia gave a mental shrug. She had abandoned propriety the moment she had left her parents' home. She would always consider herself a lady, but the binding strictures that had so consumed her life in society now seemed more than a little ridiculous.

"Very well, Sebastian."

His slow, heart-stopping smile was reward enough for her weakness, and Amelia made no protest as he reached out to gently grasp her hand in his own. The dangerous sensations tingling through her body were a worry for later.

"I brought a few guests with me. I hope you do not mind?"

"Guests?" She lifted her brow in surprise.

"Very important guests." Slowly shifting his body, he allowed Amelia to catch sight of William happily settled upon the window seat with six black kittens curled upon his lap. Her smile abruptly widened at the sight of William's unabashed pleasure.

"Oh, bless you. William has been quite anxious to know that the kittens are well. You have greatly eased his mind."

"I feared that he might be fretting," he admitted softly.

Her gaze returned to meet his watchful look. "It was kind of you to go to such an effort."

He wrinkled his nose at her sincere gratitude. "It was no effort. I simply scooped the box from the kitchen floor."

Amelia gave a choked laugh, her eyes wide with disbelief. "Never say that you have taken the kittens into your home?"

His own lips twitched with suppressed amusement. "Much over my housekeeper's protests, although I have noted she devotes considerably more effort to seeing to the comfort of those creatures than she does to my own. I am commanded to return them within the hour for their feeding."

"She sounds a lovely woman."

Sebastian gave a teasing frown. "Fah. She is a frightening old tartar who bullies me unmercifully."

Impressed far more at his kindness toward her brother than any lavish gift he might have brought for her, Amelia reached out to lightly touch his arm.

"I . . ." Her words of gratitude failed as her gaze moved over the oddly familiar features and abruptly caught sight of a half-healed cut upon his temple. There was also the unmistakable darkening of fading bruises upon his white skin. "You have been injured."

She felt him stiffen beneath her fingers before forcing a wry smile to his lips.

"It is nothing."

Her heart clenched fiercely. The thought of him being hurt brought her physical pain. As if she had taken the blows herself.

"What occurred?"

"A brief altercation in the lane."

"With whom?"

His lips twisted wryly. "I fear I did not take the time to note his identity."

Her fingers unconsciously tightened upon his arm. "Could it have been the murderer?"

"I think not," he retorted, his tones oddly clipped.

Her brows drew together. "How can you be certain?"

He breathed out a harsh sigh. "Can you not simply accept my word?"

Amelia began to bristle at his chiding words, only to realize that she was once again being unreasonable. The poor man was still healing from his wounds, and rather than offering him sympathy, she was bullying him with her suspicions.

"Yes, of course," she said with a regretful smile. "Forgive me."

His countenance swiftly softened at her apology, his hand reaching up to cover the fingers that still lay upon his arm.

"There is nothing to forgive."

"But there is," she insisted, determined to have the air cleared between them. "I have not been entirely myself lately and I fear that my concerns have made me strike out at even those who have shown me only kindness."

He stepped closer, easily trapping her in the molten silver of his eyes. "If we are confessing, then I suppose I must also admit that I can at times be unfortunately highhanded. It was not my intent to drive you away."

Her heart flip-flopped as she felt the warmth feather over her skin. Yes, he could be highhanded, but at the moment she thought she could forgive him anything as long as he promised to continue gazing at her in precisely that manner.

With an effort she attempted to collect her disappearing wits. She could not continue to simply gape at him like a looby.

"Well, now that we have that out of the way, I wish to know if you have been injured elsewhere."

"I am well." A rather strange glint of humor simmered in his eyes. "I heal remarkably quickly."

She tilted her head to one side. "I hope that your attacker was suitably punished?"

His rueful chuckle tingled down her spine. "No. To be honest, I did not give a good accounting of myself. In my defense, however, I was taken by surprise. On the next occasion I shall be better prepared."

Her breath caught. No. She could not even consider the thought of this gentleman being harmed.

"I pray there is no next time."

"As do I."

"Still, you must take better care."

His brows rose at her fierce command. "Lectures from the daring Amelia Hadwell?"

In spite of herself, Amelia felt a renegade tug of amusement at her lips. It was perhaps a bit hypocritical to command him to keep himself safe when she had blatantly announced she was going to hunt for a murderer.

"I am not the one nursing cuts and bruises, sir."

The silver eyes widened before he gave a swift laugh. "I suppose I walked straight into that one?"

Her smile widened in enjoyment at his teasing. "As a matter of fact, you did."

He became still as he gazed down at her upturned face. Then he slowly shook his head.

"Amazing."

The breathless sensation returned as she battled to slow the sudden charge of her heart.

"What?"

His hand lifted to gently touch the corner of her mouth, seemingly unaware that he was making her knees so weak she could barely stand.

"I did not realize how extraordinarily charming dimples could be."

"You are being absurd," she breathed.

He heaved a barely perceptible sigh. "It appears to be my fate when you are near."

"Sebastian . . ."

The desire to confess that he managed to confuse and befuddle her with equal force was abruptly snatched away as Mrs. Benson entered the room with a beaming smile.

"Here we are. Some nice hot tea and fresh muffins."

Six

The Gypsy stood in the darkness, her lined face wreathed in concern. "You must not falter. The danger is close, far closer than you know."

Amelia struggled to reach the woman, a sense of panic fluttering in her stomach. "What danger? Where is it?"

"It follows you. Close. So close."

"But . . . what can I do?"

The woman was fading into mist as she held out a gnarled hand. "Trust in the Guardian."

"Guardian? There is no guardian."

The Gypsy smiled. "He is watching you."

"Please, tell me of the danger."

"Protect the amulet." The voice was barely able to reach Amelia's straining ears. "You must keep it safe."

"No, do not leave. I need to know . . ."

Amelia awakened with a jerk.

Blast. Struggling to untangle from the covers that threatened to smother her, Amelia groaned in annoyance. The dream haunted her without mercy. No matter how tired she might be, at some point during the night she was destined to be visited by the relentless Gypsy.

At last able to sit upright, Amelia instinctively reached up to touch the amulet about her neck. She should simply toss away the necklace and be done with it, she thought with a weary yawn. Perhaps then she would be allowed a night without the disturbing presence of the old Gypsy.

Oddly, however, she knew that she would do no such thing. There was something comforting about the heavy weight of the amulet as it nestled against her skin. Almost as if it belonged there in some indefinable manner.

With a shake of her head at her fuzzy thoughts, Amelia prepared to return beneath the covers when a familiar tingle of excitement drifted down her spine.

On this occasion she did not dismiss the vague warning. She knew precisely what it meant.

Not giving herself time for second thoughts, she slipped from the bed and grabbed her nightrail from a nearby chair. Pulling it over her gown, she quietly left her room and made her way through the sleeping house.

Using the experience that she had gained during her past forays in the dark, she managed to avoid the occasional steps that creaked and the tables that littered the hall. She even kept the number of times she banged her toes to less than a dozen.

All the time the tingles grew more pronounced and warmth began to flood through her blood. She was growing nearer, she acknowledged with a twitch of her heart. Much nearer.

At last slipping through the kitchen door, Amelia paused only a moment before moving through the small garden toward a large oak tree.

"Sebastian," she called softly.

"I am here." There was only a moment of hesitation before a darker shadow detached from the low wall about the garden and stepped into the bright, silver moonlight. "I thought you would be sleeping."

Amelia discovered her gaze clinging to the chiseled lines of his features and the broad width of his shoulders, as if she had not seen him only yesterday. She knew she could stand there and simply drink in his male beauty for hours if it would not make her appear noddy.

"I was," she finally forced out in husky tones.

He moved toward her with a slow, fluid grace, almost as if afraid a sudden movement might send her into flight.

"Surely I was not so clumsy as to waken you?"

"No." She breathed in deeply, taking pleasure in that warm scent of male skin and the faint hint of spice. "It is odd. Somehow I seemed to sense you were here."

"Perhaps not so odd."

She tilted her head back to meet his silver gaze squarely. "What are you doing here?"

He lifted his slender, elegant hands. "Admiring the beauty of the night."

"You could not admire the beauty of the night from your own garden?" she teased gently.

He gave a rueful shrug. "It seemed prudent to ensure that William had not decided upon a midnight stroll."

She had known precisely why he was there, but his confession still sent a warmth flooding her heart. She was unaccustomed to anyone taking such concern for her brother, or herself. Not even her parents.

Her hand reached out of its own accord to touch his arm. "That is very thoughtful, Sebastian, but you should not feel obligated to keep a watch upon William. He is my responsibility."

"I do not feel obligated, Amelia." He searched her face bathed in moonlight. "I am here because I desire to be."

"Oh."

His lips twitched at her obvious bemusement. "I do regret, however, that I awakened you, no matter how unintentionally."

Amelia did not. Standing in the silvered darkness of the garden and surrounded by the pungent aroma of roses, she thought that she must still be dreaming.

A handsome, charming gentleman. A moonlit night. The seductive privacy of a garden.

It was all far too romantic for an aging, nearly-upon-the-shelf spinster.

"I do not mind." She offered him a tentative smile. "It is a lovely night."

He nodded slowly but his gaze never left her.

"A magical night."

"Magical?"

His hand lifted to lightly touch the raven curls that tumbled about her shoulders.

"The moon is full and there is bewitchment in the air."

There was certainly bewitchment, but Amelia was quite certain it had more to do with the tall gentleman standing before her than the moon.

"You surely do not believe in such nonsense?"

His brows lifted. "Why do you condemn it as non-sense? Civilizations have honored the power of the moon for centuries. Indeed, most cultures worshipped it as a god."

"Or goddess," she readily pointed out.

"Certainly." He smiled deep into her eyes. "I have al-ways presumed the moon's seductive lure must be that of a female. Still, in the old days Hindus believed that it was a very male god of the moon who would ride through the sky in a chariot pulled by white horses." His low chuckle echoed through the still air. "And, of course, they thought the moon itself a storehouse of elixir that the gods would drink, causing it to become smaller with every passing night."

Amelia discovered herself intrigued despite the fact that she had never been fond of studies.

"A rather odd belief."

"Ah, perhaps you would prefer the ancient Samarians, who thought the moon a young, handsome bull with long horns whom they named Sin."

"Sin." Her eyes suddenly twinkled with humor. "Somehow that seems a rather appropriate name."

"Indeed." His fingers moved to trace the line of her brow, sending a shock of sensations through her body. "Nights such as this lead to all sorts of wicked thoughts."

Wicked. Amelia shivered, feeling oddly unlike herself in the darkened garden. Perhaps it was the moonlight. Or the delicious scent of roses. Or perhaps this was simply a moment out of time, she thought dizzily. Whatever the reason, she desperately longed to shrug aside her heavy burdens and responsibilities. Just for now she wanted to be a young, beautiful maiden with nothing to concern her but a very desirable flirtation with a handsome gentleman.

With a deliberate coyness she peered at him from beneath her heavy lashes.

"You intrigue me, sir. What possible wicked thoughts could a gentleman such as you possess?"

His breath rasped through the air at her deliberately provoking manner, but his expression never altered.

"Thoughts best forgotten, my dear."

"Why?"

"You do enjoy playing with fire, do you not?" he murmured, his fingers moving to outline the full curve of her lips.

"At times, I suppose." Lost in the unfamiliar fever

that seared her blood, Amelia shifted close enough to feel his body through the thin lawn of her gown. "Do you prefer the more cautious paths?"

He gave a choked groan deep in his throat, his fingers convulsively cupping her cheek. "They are considerably safer."

"But often dull."

"And peaceful."

She gazed into the eyes that had turned to a misty smoke. "Surely as a scholar you desire some stimulation to keep your wits sharp?"

His features remained composed, but Amelia could sense the rapid, uneven beat of his heart. He might desire to be indifferent but his body was swiftly betraying him.

"It depends entirely upon the stimulation," he muttered. "My wits do not feel particularly sharp at the moment."

Her smile was filled with a feminine mystery as old as time. Oh no, at this moment she was not boring, responsible Amelia Hadwell at all.

"Perhaps you should blame it upon the moon."

"The moon does indeed possess its share of blame." His gaze lowered to where his fingers continued to brush over her lips. "But not all, I think."

"I have no ancient powers."

His expression became wry. "You are mistaken. Your powers are the most ancient of all."

A faint frown touched her brow as she sensed the rigid control that wrapped about his inner passions.

"Powers you are quite determined to resist, are you not?"

He drew in a deep, uneven breath, an unmistakable flare of pain darkening his eyes.

"It seems the wisest course."

"Why?"

"There is still a demon haunting the neighborhood. As long as there is danger then I must remain vigilant." His hand tightened upon her cheek, his expression somber. "It is very important, Amelia."

"Yes, I know," she agreed softly, even as her mind shied from recalling such unpleasantness. There would be time enough for such worries tomorrow.

Clearly sensing her dangerous mood, Sebastian shifted uneasily. "You should return to bed."

Her fingers tightened upon his arm. "I am not tired. I feel . . . I do not know, as if my blood is on fire."

A fine shiver raced through him. A shiver echoed within herself.

"Moon madness," he whispered.

"Perhaps the moon does have its share of blame, but not all," she softly echoed his own words.

"Amelia," he moaned in agonized tones.

Emboldened by the undeniable desire smoldering in his eyes, Amelia leaned even closer to his welcome strength. Moon madness or not, she was not yet prepared for this interlude to end.

"Do you desire to kiss me?"

Sebastian stiffened, and for a horrified moment she thought she might have disgusted him with her forward behavior. He was no doubt a gentleman unaccustomed to such giddy recklessness. Then he shifted so he could frame her face with his hands. Even in the moonlight she could easily detect the strain upon his countenance.

"You can have no notion," he breathed.

Her heart fluttered. "Then why do you not?"

"As I said, it is not wise."

Her own hands rose to cover his fingers still cupping her face. The tingling excitement in the air could not be denied.

"For the moment I do not wish to be wise. The

moon is shining, the roses are blooming, and I am an aging spinster who has never been kissed."

"Hardly a spinster," he growled.

"I am three-and-twenty, near enough to be put upon the shelf."

"Absurd." His gaze stroked over her countenance, lingering for a long moment upon the unsteady line of her mouth. She could feel the taut control that hardened his body. "You are young and beautiful and utterly enchanting. If you desire to be kissed I do not doubt that gentlemen will be beating a path to your door."

Amelia could not stop her short, almost bitter laugh. "You know little of gentlemen if you believe they are interested in a maiden who has firmly turned her back upon society and devotes most of her attention to a brother most would consider mad."

Sebastian frowned, as if displeased with the stark truth she had accepted long ago.

"A gentleman of sense would surely rejoice at being well rid of society and delighted by your unwavering loyalty. Do not sell yourself short, my dear."

She realized that he was simply attempting to make her feel better. It was his nature. But at the moment she did not want sympathy or vague reassurances.

"Obviously I have yet to meet a gentleman of sense," she retorted in low tones.

Sebastian sucked in a deep breath, his head lowering until his forehead touched her own.

"Oh, Amelia, you are surely destined to shatter my peaceful existence."

He was so wondrously close. Near enough to make her entire body quiver with longing. Amelia could resist temptation no longer. She wanted to know how it felt to be held in this man's arms and kissed by those lips that she had thought of far too often over the past few days.

Perhaps she was too reckless and impulsive, but she was quite certain that unless she did something desperate, Sebastian's rigid self-control would remain intact until the end of time.

Not giving herself time for second thoughts, Amelia lifted her hands until she could plunge her fingers into the thick silk of his hair. At the same moment she tilted her head so she could press her lips softly to his own.

At first the pure shock of pleasure that raced through her overrode every other sensation. The garden, the night, the world itself disappeared as giddy delight seared through her body. This was what a kiss was supposed to be, she thought dreamily. The heat, the racing excitement, and the dangerous stirrings deep within her.

Then, slowly, she realized that Sebastian was no longer holding himself stiffly in shock, but instead his arms had encircled her waist and he was fiercely returning her kiss.

With a moan of heady enjoyment, she leaned against the hard muscles of his chest, her hands running through the length of his hair. She could feel his shudders as he hungrily returned her kiss, and the rising tide of desire was sharply echoed within her.

She had hoped that the kiss would ease the frustration that was plaguing her, but oddly, it only seemed to fuel the restless need. She wanted to be closer, to run her hands over the hard planes of his body and to feel his fingers against her bare skin. She yearned to drown in the flood of sensations that clouded her mind and tormented her body.

It was the knowledge that her thoughts were becoming increasingly wicked that caused Amelia at last to reluctantly pull back.

"Oh," she breathed unsteadily.

His lips twitched at her obvious shock, but the silver eyes remained dark with barely suppressed desire.

"Is that all you have to say?"

Her hands moved to clutch his shoulders. It was that or sinking to the damp ground.

"It was very . . . enlightening."

Sebastian's own hands lightly trailed up and down her spine, seemingly unaware of the distracting sparks he was setting off.

"I am uncertain if that is good or bad."

"I am uncertain as well."

He was caught off guard by her blunt honesty. "Amelia, what is it?"

Sensing his growing concern, she managed a small smile. "You spoke of danger, but I did not realize precisely how potent a mere kiss could be."

She half expected him to laugh at her innocent amazement. Or even to reveal a faint smugness at his ability to stir her with such ease.

Instead, his expression was heartbreakingly tender as he gazed deep into her wide eyes.

"Nor did I."

She regarded him with a faint frown. "But you have kissed before."

His hand shifted to lightly stroke her cheek. "Ah, but I have not kissed you before." He drew in a deep breath. "Now I must firmly insist that you return to your bed while I am still able to allow you to go alone."

On this occasion she did not give her reckless streak an opportunity to protest. She had tasted the fire. She could only hope that she had not yet become addicted.

"Good night, Sebastian."

He briefly lowered his head to brush a kiss over her forehead before pulling away.

"Good night, my dear."

Sebastian watched Amelia hurry through the garden with a wrenching sense of loss.

He had known from the moment she had entered the garden that he should leave. He had only been at the house to ensure that there were no unwelcome visits from Drake. And, of course, to keep an eye open for the mysterious vampire who had attacked him in the stables.

He had not expected to have Amelia make a sudden appearance. And certainly he had not expected her to so easily slip beneath his stern self-control.

Still, he was all too aware that his passions ran far too hot during the silky darkness of the night. And combined with his growing awareness of the maiden, it had been the makings of a disaster from the beginning.

Yes, he should have left, he acknowledged as he thrust his hands through his mussed hair. But deep within his logical self-reproach there remained a shimmering pleasure that refused to regret the interlude.

The deepening bonds that were being woven between the two of them had only intensified the passions that threatened to blaze out of control. Each sensation was shared. Each need echoed within the other.

But beyond that was the more dangerous realization that she was beginning to consume more than just his passions. He admired that bright, impetuous nature. The staunch courage that she revealed in establishing her own home. And the tender care that she devoted to her brother.

She was a rare, sometimes aggravating minx who continually rattled him out of his stoic existence.

Lost in thought, Sebastian barely had time before the familiar prickle of warning raced over his skin. In one sweeping motion he had reached beneath his jacket to remove the deadly dagger and turned to confront the golden-haired vampire regarding him with mocking disdain.

"So very touching, Sebastian."

"Drake."

Taking a step closer, the vampire allowed his icy gaze to flick over Sebastian.

"You know, you are an insult to all vampires," he drawled. "'Tis embarrassing enough that you do not feast upon such a delectable morsel, but to actually turn aside her obvious desire to be ravished is shameful."

Sebastian lifted the dagger before swiftly regaining his composure. No. He could not allow himself to be goaded. He needed his wits sharply clear. This vampire was a traitor. And perhaps was in league with the deadly attacker who had so readily used forbidden methods. One moment of distraction and he might be destroyed.

Leaving Amelia alone to face the desperate renegade.

An unbearable thought.

"Thankfully, the majority of vampires have gained command of their more savage impulses," he retorted in cold tones.

Drake gave a rasping laugh. "Fah. They have become spineless eunuchs."

"You believe scavenging in dark alleys like an animal is a superior existence?"

The overly pretty features abruptly hardened at Sebastian's well-aimed thrust.

"Scavenging? You fool. I have been gaining power.

Powers that are a vampire's right. Would you care for a taste of my newfound strength?"

Sebastian shrugged a shoulder. "You do not frighten me, Drake."

"That is because you do not know what you face." A hard smile touched the thin lips. "Soon enough you will be eager to join me."

Drake's decided edge of smugness made Sebastian abruptly still. He had always been arrogant and certain of his superiority over all. But Sebastian sensed that now it was more than mere arrogance.

He slowly narrowed his gaze. "Because of the mysterious renegade who assists you?"

Abruptly realizing that he had perhaps given more away than he had intended, Drake determinedly returned the sneer to his face. That in itself was enough to convince Sebastian that the vampire was well aware of the mysterious assailant.

"I need no assistance. Certainly not to overcome one of your pathetic abilities."

So, he wished to deny the connection. Perhaps there was something here that he could use to his advantage.

With an effort, Sebastian managed a faint smile. "Clearly your cohort is not so confident in your glorious powers. He attempted to take matters into his own hands."

Drake could not hide his shock. "You were attacked?"

"Yes. Perhaps you should keep a closer leash upon the villain if you wish to be the one to better me."

It took a moment before Drake was turning away to hide his expression. "Perhaps your brothers have come to the same conclusion as myself and have decided you are an appalling specimen for a vampire."

"Or perhaps your fellow traitor has decided he does not desire to share the powers of the Medallion."

With a growl, Drake whirled back to face Sebastian with deadly anger. "I should kill you now."

Sebastian held the dagger ready. "You are welcome to try."

"You believe that absurd dagger will save you?"

"We shall soon discover," Sebastian retorted with grim determination.

Drake hesitated, seemingly debating within himself before giving a harsh laugh.

"You tempt me, Sebastian, but luckily for you I have more pressing concerns this night. Consider this a gift. On the next occasion I will not be so kindly disposed."

Sebastian regarded him steadily, forcing himself to put aside his fear for Amelia and even his lingering fury at being so ruthlessly attacked. This was a vampire. A brother.

"And then what? Drake, you are not unintelligent. Nefri and the other vampires will never allow you to gain command of the Medallion."

A snarl twisted the handsome features. "They will have no choice."

"No." Sebastian gave a slow shake of his head. "You fight a losing battle. Still, it is not too late to give up this madness and return to the Veil."

"I am no eunuch." He stepped back, his arrogance shimmering in the air about him. "You may be satisfied with your cold bed and dusty books, but I am destined for far greater rewards."

There was a sudden chill in the breeze before Drake was abruptly shape-shifting into a dark shadow that disappeared down the lane in the blink of an eye.

Sebastian made no effort to follow the renegade. He knew where to find his lair, if the time became necessary. Instead he remained standing at the edge of the garden with a frown upon his brow.

There was something he was missing, he realized with a pang of aggravation at his unusual lack of perception. Drake was always overly confident and certain of his powers. Even behind the Veil. But whatever his arrogance, he was not without some sense.

Why was he willing to risk utter destruction when he must know that there would be others who hastened to stop him? He could not battle every vampire. Not even with the Medallion.

So what did he know that Sebastian didn't?

And what did it have to do with his mysterious companion?

And how dangerous was it not knowing the answer to those questions?

Seven

Drake paced the cramped cottage with quick, restless steps. He was furious. More than furious.

He was no dupe, he told himself savagely. Nor was he a fool.

When he had left the Veil it was clearly understood that it would be his task to retrieve the Medallion. As well as to put a stop to Sebastian, or any of the other vampires, if they should stand in his path.

To have this sudden interference was unbearable. And more than a bit suspicious.

If the plans had changed he should have been consulted. He would not be left dangling as bait while the prize was snatched from beneath his very nose.

Oh no, he would not tolerate such blatant interference.

He turned about and abruptly froze. The approaching sense of the vampire was filling the dark, dank air and Drake swiftly smoothed his hands over his fine emerald jacket. It was about bloody time, he seethed. He had been waiting at this hideous cottage for near three hours.

Holding himself steady, he watched the fog thicken and swirl beneath the door, shimmering in the darkness with an evil glow of its own.

"At last . . ." he began to complain, only to have his

words roughly choked off as the fog reached out to wrap about his neck. For long, agonizing moments he was held in its ruthless grip, his feet actually leaving the dusty floor before at last he was tossed disdainfully against a wall.

"Never," the fog rasped, "never summon me in such a manner again."

With painful movements, Drake forced himself back to his feet, his fury now mixed with fear. How he longed to put an end to this vampire, he seethed with black hatred. A slow, torturous end.

"I had to speak with you," he said in a tone roughened by his aching throat.

The fog stirred the dust restlessly upon the floor. "You risked exposing my presence to Nefri, you dolt. Not to mention alerting the Great Council that I have discovered a means of traveling through the Veil undetected."

Drake clenched his hands at his side. Dolt? No one called him a dolt.

"It would not have been necessary had you not lied to me."

The words seemed to ring in the air for a nerve-wracking moment before the fog shifted in a foreboding manner.

"Lied? You have become overly bold, Drake. Take care I am not forced to teach you a rather unpleasant lesson in humility."

In spite of himself, Drake felt himself pressing closer to the moldy wall.

"Did you attempt to destroy Sebastian?"

"You must be confused. I do not answer to you."

"I believe I have earned the right to some explanation. You requested that I leave the Veil to retrieve the Medallion. You also specifically warned me that it would be my duty to ensure that Sebastian did not pose a problem. Have you altered your plans?"

The low laugh sent a chill down Drake's spine. "Do you mean, have I chosen to retrieve the Medallion without your incompetent assistance?"

Drake silently added the insult to the list of others, reassuring himself that his sweet revenge would come the moment he held the Medallion.

As long as he gained command of the artifact. At the moment that was all that was important.

"Yes."

"It is a temptation, I must admit," the vampire drawled. "I chose what I thought to be three ruthless hunters and was rewarded with cowardly fools."

"I am no coward," Drake snapped.

"Ah, then you have retrieved the amulet?"

"Not as yet, but I will have it in my hands within a few days."

The vampire gave a disgusted grunt. "The same promise made by both Amadeus and Tristan before they were destroyed."

Drake shrugged off the words. He did not desire to be compared with such fools.

"I will not fail."

"That remains to be seen."

He hardened his features in grim determination. "You have not answered my question. Do you seek to retrieve the Medallion for yourself?"

The fog shifted, but even as Drake stiffened in fear, it deliberately settled in the center of the room.

"If that was my desire, then the Medallion would be mine."

Drake cautiously released the breath he had unconsciously sucked in. "Then why did you attack Sebastian?"

"You try your luck, Drake. My actions are not your concern."

"I have put myself at considerable risk for you."

"With the promise of great power as a reward," the fog hissed in return.

Drake tilted his chin, although he was careful to keep himself firmly against the wall.

"Only if you do not decide to withhold the rewards."

That horrid, rasping laugh once again echoed through the cottage, sending the few remaining rats scurrying into the night.

"Do not fear, Drake. You shall be suitably rewarded for your efforts. My only interest in Sebastian was to lure Nefri from her lair. A scheme that worked to perfection, I might add."

Drake frowned. He did not like to recall that Nefri might be near. He could not possibly hope to match the ancient vampire's powers. Perhaps not even with the Medallion in hand.

"Nefri?" he muttered.

"Yes. Surely you have not forgotten that she continues to lurk near the maidens who hold the Medallion?"

He shifted uneasily. "Of course I have not forgotten. You promised she would not interfere."

"And she will not, as long as you do not ruin all with your childish fits of hysteria."

Hysteria? The vampire went too far. Drake narrowed his gaze. "Perhaps if you would warn me of your intentions . . ."

In the blink of an eye the fog was once again striking out, clenching about Drake's throat until it threatened to crush it.

"Enough." The voice was frozen steel. "I will decide

what you will or will not be told. Do not make the mistake of questioning me again."

Drake struggled to remain conscious, well aware that he had pressed the vampire too far. Damn. He did not doubt the elder would dispose of him without a flicker of remorse.

"No, I understand. I will not question you again," he choked out in desperation.

The crushing grip remained. "And Drake, my patience wears thin. Retrieve the Medallion or you will wish that you *could* be simply destroyed."

"I . . . I will have it."

"Cats, cats, cats."

William was nearly bouncing up and down as the thin, rather dour-faced housekeeper shifted the large box from the counter and placed it upon the floor.

"Yes. Now sit down before you stomp 'em to bits," the woman muttered, although there was no missing the pleased glint in the pale blue eyes.

Standing on the far side of the kitchen, Amelia smiled. After a morning devoted to listening to William's disgruntled sighs and watching him wander through the house with restless frustration, she had realized she must do something to distract him.

The poor boy simply could not understand her insistence that he not visit the children in the stews, nor why he could not even stroll through the market. It was little wonder that he chafed at her restrictions.

At last, in desperation, she had made the bold decision to bring him to Sebastian's home to visit the kittens. She knew that was one certain way to distract him for at least an hour. And perhaps it would make him somewhat more content for the rest of the day.

And, of course, a tiny voice whispered in the back

of her mind, she was not being entirely selfless. If she were being perfectly honest with herself this was precisely where she desired to be.

A renegade heat flared beneath her cheeks as she recalled her encounter with Sebastian in the garden.

It had been wicked. And dangerous. Far more dangerous than she ever could have suspected.

But it had also been the most glorious few moments in her life. And whether it made her a horrible person or not, she could not deny that she could not wait for another opportunity to taste passion once again.

She was perhaps shameless, and bold beyond reproach, but that did not keep her from imagining the feel of his hard arms and seeking lips. Oh yes, she was very anxious to flirt with the wicked peril once again.

Almost as if her siren's call had lured Sebastian through the large town house, Amelia felt the tingles that warned her of his approach. With little shame, she deliberately shifted until she was near the door. She had known he would come. That he would sense her presence as easily as she sensed his.

Quite prepared when he at last approached through the shadows, Amelia nevertheless found her breath being caught in her throat as her gaze skimmed over the silver gray coat and burgundy waistcoat. He wore high, glossy boots, and his thick hair was tied at the nape of his neck, as if he had been out riding. Then, compulsively, she was seeking the pale beauty of his countenance, searching for some reaction to her decidedly brash behavior.

What she discovered made her breath even more elusive. Halting directly at her side, he offered a slow, tantalizing smile.

"Amelia."

"Sebastian." A ridiculous bout of nerves had her unnecessarily smoothing the soft folds of her blue gown.

"I hope you do not mind our intrusion. William was bored and demanding to be out of the house. I thought the kittens might prove to be an adequate distraction."

"I do not mind," he murmured, his silver gaze never straying from her face. "Would you care to join me in the library?"

"Well . . ." She reluctantly turned to regard her brother as he played with the kittens.

"My housekeeper will keep a careful watch on William," he softly assured her.

She hesitated another moment, knowing how her brother could fret if she were absent, but then noting his obvious distraction and the way the housekeeper hovered protectively at his side. She slowly turned to offer Sebastian a smile.

"Very well."

Reaching out, Sebastian firmly placed her hand upon his arm and led her from the room. In silence they wound their way through the narrow halls in the servants' quarters and up the stairs that would take them to the front of the house.

Although vibrantly aware of the man at her side, Amelia could not help but note the decided lack of ornaments upon the paneled walls and occasional tables. And she would have to be blind not to see the heavy covers that continued to hide the chairs set in the alcoves.

A smile twitched at her lips. She wondered if Sebastian even took a moment to notice his surroundings.

"Why do you smile?" he demanded.

Tilting her face upward, Amelia met the amused gaze. "I was thinking that only a bachelor could bear to live among dust sheets and barren rooms."

"I will admit it does not trouble me as long as my library is in order."

She gave a teasing click of her tongue. "Surely a man needs more in his life than books?"

The silver eyes abruptly darkened. "I have not believed so for many years."

Something in that deep, accented voice made her heart make a sudden leap. "And now?"

His smile widened. "And now a pair of dimples has made me question my simple existence."

Amelia breathed deeply of his warm, spicy scent, not at all surprised when her head swirled. This gentleman could make any poor, susceptible maiden a bit dizzy.

"Being distracted by dimples does not seem at all scholarly."

"No?" His gaze swept over her. "Well, there are all sorts of studies. Not all of them including dusty books."

She chuckled softly, her fingers tightening upon his arm. "There may be hope for you yet, Mr. St. Ives."

"Perhaps there is, Miss Hadwell." Slowing his steps, he turned her into the large library. "Here we are."

Her gaze swept over the beautiful room, lingering on the highly polished tables and the obvious care given to the hundreds of leather bound books.

"Not a dust sheet in sight," she murmured.

The silver eyes twinkled. "I could have one fetched if you would like."

"No, thank you," she retorted with a grimace.

The slender hand waved toward the pair of leather wing chairs that framed a heavy marble chimney piece. "Will you have a seat?"

Amelia found herself rather reluctant to loosen her hold upon him, but she at least retained enough sense to realize she could not remain gazing up at him like a moonling. Instead, she forced herself to calmly drop her hand and move toward the nearest chair.

She did halt as she noted the book that had been left on a small table beside one of the chairs. Picking up the heavy tome, she turned to regard Sebastian with a lift of her brows.

"What are you studying?"

"At the moment I am pursuing the writings of Epicurus."

"Ah." She wracked her memory for a moment. " 'If you wish to make Pythocles wealthy, don't give him more money; rather, reduce his desires . . .' "

Sebastian did not bother to hide his surprise. "You read the philosophers?"

She grimaced at his question. "Only under duress," she admitted. "My governess possessed the belief that a young lady should be well read and capable of entering any conversation without embarrassment."

"A worthy goal, I should think."

Amelia gave a faint shrug. She had no doubt that poor Miss Lyman had tried her best to instill her own fervent love for learning into her ungrateful student, but Amelia had never possessed the patience. Her restless energy was not suited to hours spent in the classroom.

"I far preferred to be fishing with William or sneaking into our neighbor's orchard. To be obliged to remain indoors like a proper maiden was sorely testing. I received any number of lectures for slipping from my window when I should have been practicing the pianoforte or perfecting my needlework."

"Lectures you no doubt ignored," he retorted in dry tones.

Her dimples flashed. "Upon occasion."

He gave a reluctant laugh as he moved to lean against one of the endless bookshelves. She watched his fluid movements, fascinated by the easy grace of such a large man. He would no doubt dance the waltz with the same exquisite skill.

"So you have no interest in musty books?" he demanded with a watchful gaze.

"To be honest, I have given little thought to studies since my schoolroom days." She wrinkled her nose in faint embarrassment. "I suppose you must think me a frippery maiden?"

His lips tilted at one corner. "No more than you must think me a dull and tedious fellow." He paused for a moment, his gaze briefly skimming over her mouth. "Still, there can be magic in books, just as in the moon."

Recalling the particular magic they had discovered beneath the moon, Amelia lifted her brows in teasing surprise.

"Why, Mr. St. Ives. What manner of books do you possess?"

A wicked glint entered his eyes. "Would you like to see?"

"Very well."

She paused only a moment before moving to join him beside the heavy shelves. Her ready agreement had nothing to do with a sudden scholarly interest, but simply the need to learn more of this man who so captivated her.

"My collection is quite varied." He reached out a slender hand to pluck a thin, rather battered volume from the shelf. "Here is one that you might find of interest."

"What is it?"

"A personal journal of an ancient warrior."

She readily accepted the book, opening it to discover the yellowed, crumbling pages covered with a strange spider web of script she had never seen before.

"What is this language?"

"It is a very old, mostly forgotten language of a for-gotten people." His expression was difficult to read as he gently touched the delicate book. "To most, his culture and beliefs would have seemed quite unnat-ural. But these pages speak of a man much like ourselves. He complains of the cold, the weevils in his bread, and his fear of the upcoming battle. Most of all, however, he speaks of his deep love for his wife and children, who he has been forced to leave behind. He prays every night that he be allowed to see the pre-cious beauty of his daughter's face one last time before he dies."

Amelia found her heart squeezing in compassion. The unknown man was long dead, but listening to Se-bastian's soft voice, it was almost as if she could see him within the narrow pages. Alone, scared, and des-perately missing his family. He was far more real than any of the characters from history she had been forced to study.

"How very sad," she murmured, lifting her gaze to meet the watching silver gaze. "And yet . . ."

"What?"

"His story is far more interesting than the books of glorious conquests and great leaders that I have com-mitted to memory. He seems more alive."

"Yes." His expression was one of satisfaction. As if she managed to please him with her response. "The simple story of a simple man who speaks to all."

Her eyes widened in a deliberately provoking man-ner. "Why, Sebastian, that was very nearly poetic."

"Do you think so?" he murmured, his fingers moving to softly stroke her cheek. "It must be the dimples."

She shivered, desperately wishing they were back in the dark garden rather than in a proper library where the housekeeper might walk in any moment. Perhaps then he would kiss her as she longed for him to do.

"I do not think you are nearly so dull and tedious as you desire others to believe," she murmured in tones less steady than she would have desired.

His fingers paused and Amelia could physically feel the frustrated desire that raced through his blood. It seared through him with the same intensity that burned within her. And yet, while the need was almost tangible, beneath the ache was a fierce tenderness that tugged at her heart. How could any woman resist such a combination?

Unfortunately, she was also aware that through it all was the thread of finely honed steel that was his determination. For whatever reason, he was battling to keep his emotions in check.

She swallowed her disappointment as he reluctantly turned his attention back toward the shelves.

"Let me see, what else can I tempt you with?" He touched a thick, ornately bound book. "Ah, the *Kitah al-Fawa' id.*"

It took a considerable effort to clear her clouded thoughts. Dear heavens, she must be bewitched, she thought inanely. That could be the only explanation for the utter certainty that she was connected to this man to her very soul.

"What is that?" she managed to question in doggedly light tones.

"A book on nautical technology written in 1490 by Ibn Majid, an Arab sailor."

"Ugh." She did not have to pretend her distaste. Her interest shifted toward a more intriguing book bound in handsome red leather. "What of that one?"

He lifted his brows, taking the book from the shelf and carefully opening it for her inspection. "Very fine taste, my dear. That is the *Institutio Oratoria.* It speaks of the fundamentals essential to educate the citizens of the Roman Empire."

The subject held little more appeal than nautical technology. Perhaps even less. It was the realization that the script was not in English that captured her attention.

Her own father had considered himself somewhat of a scholar. He kept a decent library, and possessed a handful of rare documents. He was even well respected for his speeches in the House of Lords. But for all his admired cleverness he could not hope to achieve the skilled intelligence of this master. She wondered if any gentleman in all of England could do so.

A hint of uncertainty shadowed her heart. Who was this Sebastian St. Ives?

"Precisely how many languages do you speak?" she demanded with a faint frown.

His smile remained but Amelia was certain there was a guarded quality to his beautiful eyes.

"No more than any well-studied gentleman."

"That is no answer."

He closed the book and placed it back on the shelf. In the process he managed to hide his expression.

"Does it truly matter?"

"It is yet another mystery that surrounds you." She regarded his profile with a searching gaze. "I know nothing of you. You do not speak of your family, or your past. I do not even know where you come from or why you settled in London."

"Perhaps we should return downstairs and ensure that William is still occupied with his kittens."

Her disquiet only increased at his obvious attempt to deflect her interest.

"What is it you hide from me, Sebastian?" she demanded in low tones.

"Only what is necessary," he retorted, slowly turning

to face her. The silver eyes held a hint of regret, but the alabaster features were set in lines that prevented any argument. "Shall we return to William?"

Amelia wanted to protest. This man fascinated her like no other. He touched her heart and stirred her passions. He invaded her soul like a conqueror of old. And yet, she knew nothing of him.

He asked for her trust, yet did not offer his own.

With a frustrated sigh she placed her fingers on his arm and allowed him to lead her from the room. She knew enough of men to realize she could not force his confidences. Until he was prepared to lower his guard and share his secrets she could do no more than stew in silence.

Walking through the shadowed hall, Amelia stewed.

Eight

The sound from the garden was faint, but distinct enough to wrench Amelia from her light sleep. With a groan she pulled the covers over her head and willed herself to return to the decidedly pleasant dream that included Sebastian St. Ives. For once there was not a nagging, strange Gypsy in sight and she intended to enjoy the fantasy.

It was, of course, a hopeless task.

She had no more than closed her eyes when the muffled squeak once again floated through the air. Aggravated beyond bearing, Amelia tossed aside the covers and stumbled from the bed.

Just one night, she grumbled beneath her breath. Just one night she desired to sleep through until morning.

Pulling on her robe, she left the darkened bedchamber and made her way downstairs. More out of habit than concern, she dodged the squeaking steps and the perilous tables as she made her way to the kitchen. Once there, she readily pulled open the door and stepped into the thick night air.

Almost absently, she sensed that it was closer to dawn than dusk, although the inky darkness still clung tenaciously. Dark enough to make her pause as she listened carefully for the noise that had awakened her.

Could it be Sebastian? Although she did not have the familiar feeling of awareness that usually warned of his presence, he had made it obvious he intended to keep a close watch upon the house. A startling, comforting knowledge for a maiden who had been determined to forge a life of independence.

A faint smile touched her lips. She hoped it was he. She would not protest another romantic interlude in the garden, with or without the moon. The magic that had flowed through her blood like honey had nothing to do with gods of the moon. It had been a bewitchment created by Sebastian alone.

Unfortunately, it was more than likely William's cat prowling through the lane. Her smile faded. Well, on this occasion she vowed not to leave the safety of the garden. The wretched stray would not lead her a merry chase on this night.

Reaching the edge of the garden, Amelia was careful to keep herself hidden behind a large elm tree as she peered into the lane.

At first the gloom seemed impossibly deep. With no moonlight, the darkness was near complete. But then, strangely, her eyes seemed to adjust to the shadows, almost as if the blackness were being filtered to gray. Astonishing.

Within a few moments, however, her astonishment shifted to an icy apprehensiveness. Just across the narrow lane she could vaguely make out the shape of a large man bent over an object on the ground.

Her hands frantically pressed against her lips, stifling the instinctive scream. Against her will, she was brutally thrust back to that horrid night when she had witnessed the shadow as it hovered over the body of that poor woman.

Was this the man who had committed the ghastly murder? Had he struck once again?

The mere thought was enough to freeze her very blood.

She had to flee, a cowardly voice whispered in the back of her mind. She had to make it back to the house before she was missed. But even as the thoughts were running through her mind, a low moan echoed through the silent air.

Dear heavens, whoever was upon the ground was still alive! And clearly in pain.

How could she possibly leave? Someone was in danger. Perhaps even now dying. If she left she would have their death upon her conscience.

Paralyzed between stark fear and the need to try to save the wounded soul, Amelia was unprepared when the crouching shape fluidly straightened, and then began to walk straight toward the tree where she was hidden.

He could not see her; she vaguely attempted to stem the raw burst of terror. She was safely concealed by the shadows. But against all logic, the looming figure paced toward her relentlessly until she felt a cold prickle crawl over her skin.

"Good evening, Miss Hadwell," a familiar, mocking voice cut through the thick silence. "You might as well come out and make your curtsy. I have been waiting for you."

Her heart wrenched to a halt as she stepped out warily, her knees so weak she knew it was useless to attempt to flee.

"Mr. Ramone," she breathed in dread.

The handsome features were cold in the oddly gray mist. Even worse, there was a dark wetness clinging to his lips. Amelia's horrified mind shied from even considering what the damp stain might be.

"Who did you expect?" Mr. Ramone demanded. "That tedious Nefri?"

Amelia blinked in fearful confusion. "Nefri?"

"No?" A sardonic expression settled upon the pale countenance. "No, of course not. It is that pathetically devoted Sebastian that you seek. I fear that he has been distracted for the moment."

Sebastian. Dear heavens, she had not even considered the thought that he might be in danger. Her heart felt as if it were being crushed by a ruthless hand.

"What have you done with him?"

"He is unharmed. For the moment, at least." An awful smile curved those wet lips. "Unfortunately, I can not say the same for his housekeeper. I fear that she might not survive."

Raw horror raced through her. "You killed that poor old woman?"

"It brought me no pleasure, I assure you." He shrugged, as casual as if they were discussing the weather, stepping closer to her trembling body. "I far prefer my sufferers to be young, ripe, and beautiful. Much like yourself."

She shuddered, stumbling backward in instinctive revulsion. At the same moment, however, Mr. Ramone's distinctive scent filled the air and she froze. That smell. A smell of cold steel. Just like . . . what?

Just like the night she had witnessed the first murder, a small voice whispered in the back of her mind.

Of course. She should have suspected the truth the moment the man had first approached her. She had sensed there was something wrong about him. Something wrong and dangerous.

"You . . . you were the shadow," she stammered before considering how dangerous confessing her awareness of his monstrous sins might be.

"Yes."

Her hands pressed to her heaving stomach. "Dear lord, what are you?"

"What am I?" He mockingly pretended to consider the question. "I am your master. The one chosen to rule above all."

"This is madness. A . . . nightmare."

"A nightmare?" His eyes narrowed to cold slits. "Truly, Miss Hadwell, there is no need to be insulting. You should consider yourself to be exceedingly fortunate. It is not every mortal who can claim to have been in the company of the most superior of all vampires."

Amelia uttered a strangled noise. She desperately desired to close her eyes and pretend this was all some horrible nightmare. Instead, she attempted to clear the fear fogging her mind.

"You must be insane. There are no such things as vampires."

"No? Would you desire me to prove the truth?" The thin lips widened to reveal the white teeth. Then, even as Amelia watched in morbid fascination, a set of fangs lengthened to glint evilly in the darkness. "I assure you I have devoted a number of nights to considering how pleasurable it would be to feast upon you."

Instinctively, Amelia lifted protective hands to her throat. It could not be possible. Vampires were myths. Mere children's stories.

But possible or not, there was no denying the awful truth.

This gentleman was a vampire. And she was standing directly in his path.

"I . . . what do you want from me?" she managed at last to choke out.

"It is rather a simple thing. I desire your amulet."

Amelia was quite certain she had misunderstood. "My amulet? Why?"

"You are hardly in a position to ask questions, my dear," he rasped.

That was certainly true enough. Only a fool would dare to cross this dangerous monster. And, a very large part of her had no desire to cross him. Not when she had only to shift her head to see the last poor victim of this vampire lying still as death upon the ground.

And yet, Amelia found herself hesitating. There had to be a reason for his desire for the amulet. No doubt a dangerous and nefarious reason. And had the Gypsy not warned her never to give the necklace to another?

Besides which, she had a horrible fear that the moment he had the necklace in hand she would be yet another maiden found savaged upon the streets of London.

"It belongs to me," she retorted between stiff lips.

She heard his rasp as he stepped even closer. "Do not be a fool. It could never belong to a mere animal. The amulet is but a piece of an ancient Medallion that belongs in the hands of a vampire. In my hands."

"No, you are mistaken," she babbled. "This was given to me by an old Gypsy woman."

"It was given to you by Nefri. An interfering, loathsome vampire who has mistakenly presumed that she is capable of forcing other vampires into becoming her willing prisoners. It is a fate I have no intention of enduring."

That sweet old woman had been a vampire? Her head whirled and her heart was beating so rapidly that she thought it might burst. Had the entire world gone mad?

"Is it enchanted?"

The thin lips twisted. "In a manner of speaking. Now, I will have it."

Her hand clutched the amulet. "No."

"Fool." A savage anger twisted the elegant features and the vampire lifted his hands, as if to take the necklace by force. Then, to Amelia's vast relief, the sudden glow of approaching lanterns brought the stalker to a halt.

Covertly glancing out of the corner of her eye, she noted the small group of men determinedly headed down the alley. Their obvious lack of stealth and steady pace clearly indicated their identity at once.

"The Watch," she breathed in unsteady tones.

She heard the vampire growl, but his expression remained one of evil intent. "You think I fear any mortal? They are mere fodder." He paused for a long moment. "Still, they do have their uses."

Amelia eyed him in wary terror. Could he possibly kill so many? Or was he simply attempting to keep her from calling out for help?

"What uses?"

Without warning, the monster reached beneath his coat to remove a long, blue scarf.

"A little memento I intend to leave upon my latest morsel."

"A scarf?"

His soft laughter was more horrifying than his earlier threats.

"A scarf quite exquisitely embroidered with your brother's name."

Amelia grasped the tree to keep herself from falling to the ground in fear. She, of course, now recognized the scarf. She had given it to William for his birthday only months ago. Gads, she had even been the one to embroider his name upon it.

"You beast," she hissed in fury.

"If you desire to save your brother from the hangman, you will bring me the amulet. You know where to find me."

Before Amelia could even form an answer there was a cold chill in the air and the man before her was suddenly cloaked in a heavy shadow.

"No . . ."

She stepped forward, but she already knew it was too late. Although she could make out no more than a fluid blackness as it moved toward the unmoving form on the ground, she knew beyond a doubt it was Mr. Ramone as he placed the scarf upon his victim. Even worse, the lanterns were far too close for her to have even a small chance of darting from behind the tree and retrieving the incriminating evidence without being seen.

Surely it would only make William appear even more guilty if she were seen taking the scarf away?

Dazed with shock, fear, and a blossoming dread, Amelia simply watched as the approaching men neared.

Dear lord, what was she to do?

Sebastian returned to his home in a dark fury.

He longed to indulge the passions that pulsed through his blood. To stalk the streets fiercely until he had his hands on Drake. Preferably about his neck.

Instead, he walked into the kitchen and restlessly paced the confines of the narrow kitchen.

He had been a fool, he acknowledged grimly. For all his concern for Amelia, and even for himself, he had never once thought that Drake would strike at him through his innocent housekeeper.

But then again, why should he? There was no obvious gain to be made by such a ruthless act. The servant had been unaware of his true nature, as well as Drake's. And certainly she had no interest in the Medallion.

Bloody hell. Why would Drake have lured the elderly woman to the very midst of the stews? And more to the point, why would he have left her hovering near death to suffer for hours as the last of the blood slowly drained from her body?

Was it a warning? If so, it had been utterly un-necessary.

Or had it been an attempt to distract him? And if so, from what?

The question continued to gnaw at him as he paced from the heavy table to the rack of drying herbs. It was not until a sudden intuition about Amelia permeated his body that he came to an abrupt halt. Something was wrong. He could sense her sharp discomfort, as her presence grew ever closer.

With swift movements he was at the door and pulling it open to watch as the maiden rushed through his narrow garden with her obviously reluctant brother in tow.

"Amelia," he called softly, instinctively searching for any hint of Drake in the vicinity. There was a faint sense of him in the distance, but nothing that could threaten Amelia at the moment.

He stepped aside as she continued to bowl forward, not pausing until she was through the door and steer-ing her sleepy brother toward the table. Even then she continued to fuss over her brother, pulling open a large bag she had set beside the chair and placing a battered blanket about his shoulders.

"William, I need you to stay here while I speak with Mr. St. Ives," she said in low tones.

"William tired," the boy muttered, laying his head upon the table.

Sebastian's heart gave an odd twitch as he watched Amelia reach out to softly stroke her brother's hair.

"I know, darling. Just rest here for a bit and I will soon be back."

Slowly straightening, Amelia turned to meet Sebastian's worried gaze. He had only to note the

pallor of her complexion and the unmistakable glitter
of fear in her beautiful eyes to have him abruptly
striding forward to take her hands in his own.

"Amelia." A soft snore from William stirred the
thick air and with an impatient glance at the sleeping
young man, he pulled Amelia's arm through his own.
"Come with me."

In silence they moved through the dark house,
heading directly for the library. Once there, he pressed
her into a chair and swiftly poured a large measure of
brandy. Returning with the filled glass, he pressed it
into her nerveless fingers and crouched beside the
chair so he could closely watch her tense features.

"Tell me, my dear, what has happened?"

She sucked in a shuddering breath. "It was . . . Mr.
Ramone."

Sebastian bit back the curses that threatened to spill
from his lips. "What has he done? Did he harm you?"

"No, I am well."

She did not sound as if she were well. It did not take
the heightened senses of a vampire to hear the raw
panic in her voice.

"Bloody hell." Sebastian shoved a hand through the
hair that lay loose about his shoulders. "I should have
known it was a trap from the beginning."

Surprisingly, a hint of sympathy touched the pale
face. "Your housekeeper?"

"Yes. She is gone."

Amelia reached out a hand to lightly touch his arm.
"Oh, Sebastian, I am sorry."

He shook his head. He would have to save his regrets
for later. For now he had to concentrate upon Amelia.

"Tell me of Mr. Ramone. What did he do?"

There was a short pause as she took a deep drink
of the brandy, coughing and sputtering as the fiery

liquid slid down her throat. At last she lifted her haunted gaze.

"I was in bed when I heard a noise in the garden. I went out to see what was occurring."

"Damn it all, Amelia," he burst out before he could stop the words. "When will you learn a measure of caution?"

Her lips thinned at his frustrated chiding. "It is very fortunate that I did go out to investigate. Mr. Ramone was there and he . . ."

The words stumbled to a halt and Sebastian's brief flare of annoyance faded at her barely hidden distress.

"What is it?"

"I think he had just murdered another young woman."

"Oh, Amelia." He reached up to cover the fingers that still lingered upon his arm. "I am sorry you had to witness such a ghastly thing."

"It was horrible." A shudder raced through her body. "I do not think I have ever been so frightened."

Sebastian frowned, struck by a pang of guilt. "I should have been there. What did he do?"

She shook her head, as if attempting to rid herself of the horrible memory.

"I was hidden behind the tree, but somehow he seemed to know I was there. He turned and came toward me and I could see the blood upon his lips. He was drinking her blood."

"Oh, my dear."

There was a wrenching silence before she met his steady gaze. "Did you know, Sebastian?"

He stiffened at the unexpected question. "Know?"

"That he is a vampire," she demanded, closely regarding his expression. Far too closely, he ruefully acknowledged, as her eyes slowly widened. "You did."

Sebastian grimaced, realizing it would be impossible

to lie. Damn Drake. His revelation threatened to reveal the truth about himself. Just when she needed to trust in him the most.

"Yes."

"How?" Her fingers tightened upon his arm. "How did you know?"

"That is something we can discuss later," he forced himself to say in firm tones. "For now, I need to know what occurred."

She shivered as she pressed deeper into the soft leather of her seat. "He admitted that he was the one who had committed the murders. Then, he told me he wanted my amulet."

"Your amulet?"

Her brows furrowed together. "He claimed that it was a piece of some Medallion that belongs to the vampires."

His glance instinctively lowered to where the amulet glowed against her pale skin. Pale skin that was all too temptingly revealed by her thin nightrail.

"I note that you did not give it to him."

Her expression hardened abruptly. "I wish I had."

The fierce words sent a chill down Sebastian's spine. That was the one thing he could not allow. He swiftly lifted his gaze to study her glittering eyes.

"What did he do to you, Amelia?"

"He heard the Watch approaching and before I could stop him, he had pulled out a scarf and left it upon the dead body."

"What manner of scarf?"

The dark eyes glistened with tears. "One that I had given to William for his birthday. It has his name embroidered upon it."

Sebastian sat back on his heels. Blessed Nefri. Drake had clearly known precisely where to strike. This maiden would give up everything, including her own soul, if it would save her brother from the gallows.

"I see," he muttered.

Her shoulders trembled as she battled to control her chaotic emotions. "I dared not attempt to retrieve the scarf. If they had spotted me, it would only have made them certain William was guilty."

Gently he reached for the forgotten glass of brandy and set it aside, and then, careful not to startle her, he grasped her cold hands in the warmth of his own.

"You did right, Amelia."

A lone tear slid down her pale cheek. "Did I? Once the Watch discovers that scarf they will come for my brother. I knew that I could not stop them this time. They would take him away and there was nothing I could do."

Sebastian squeezed her fingers, fiercely regretting the fearful misery etched upon her countenance. At the moment he would have gladly thrashed Drake Ramone. And Nefri as well, for ever having forced Amelia into such danger.

"But you did do something," he said softly. "You came to me."

She glanced briefly about the shadowy library, as if not quite certain what had prompted her to flee so hastily to his home. Silently he willed his own strength to bolster her flagging courage.

"I did not know where else to turn. I simply packed a few belongings and told Mrs. Benson to inform anyone who might call that William and I left London yesterday to visit my parents."

"Quite clever of you, my dear," he assured her.

"But now what?" With an effort she attempted to gather her badly shattered nerves. "We cannot simply remain here forever."

Quickly rising to his feet, Sebastian firmly tugged

her hands until she was standing before him. With great care he wrapped his arms about her and rested his cheek upon the top of her hair.

He deeply disliked seeing her so weary and frightened. He preferred his brave, proud Amelia with the flashing dimples and stubborn determination.

"That will not be necessary, I assure you, my dear," he soothed in low tones. "For tonight just know that you are safe."

A shudder raced through her as she laid her head against his chest. "Yes."

He breathed in deeply of her fresh, tantalizing scent. She felt small and dangerously fragile pressed next to his much larger frame, but it was somehow . . . right. As if he had just been made complete in a manner he had never before comprehended.

For long moments he simply held her close, marveling at the golden warmth swirling through his body. A warmth that had nothing to do with lust, or the thrill of a hunter who had captured his prey. This tender heat was far more powerful. And far more dangerous.

He thrust aside the disturbing notion.

"I will protect you, Amelia," he swore, his arms instinctively tightening. "That I promise you."

She tilted her head back to look into his darkened eyes. "Sebastian?"

"Just relax," he urged. "You do not have to be strong now. Do you want more brandy?"

"No." She regarded him for a long moment before uneasily wetting her lips. "Sebastian, I want . . . no, I *need* the truth. I cannot bear the horrible uncertainty any longer."

Sebastian regarded her warily. He had known from the moment that she had revealed her knowledge of Drake that soon enough she would question his own purpose in London. She was too intelligent not to realize there had to be some connection.

And yet, he still found himself hesitating.

He told himself it was because he feared that she would no longer trust him. That perhaps she might flee from him and expose herself to even more danger.

But he knew that was not the entire truth.

The fear ran much deeper. And perilously close to his heart.

"What truth?" he at last managed to inquire in husky tones.

"Who are you?"

Nine

Sebastian discovered himself floundering beneath her serious gaze. How the blazes did he answer such a question?

That he was a scholar? A student of philosophy who until the past few weeks had preferred to observe life from a distance rather than tossing himself in the messy business? That he was an immortal vampire? A dark, passionate monster who could destroy her with ridiculous ease?

Or that he was a gentleman who was growing increasingly enchanted with her sweetness?

In the end he made a cowardly attempt to prolong the inevitable.

"I have not lied to you, Amelia," he said in careful tones. "I am truly Sebastian St. Ives."

A faint frown tugged at her brows. "But you have revealed nothing else."

"What do you wish to know?"

Her gaze searched his face, as if seeking to discern whether he could be trusted or not.

"You will answer my questions?"

"To the best of my ability."

There was a long pause before she firmly pulled herself from his grasp and crossed her arms protectively about her waist. Sebastian experienced a pang of loss without her warmth next to him. With an effort he battled the urge to swoop forward and return her to where she obviously belonged. Perhaps it would be for the best not to have his head clouded with the passion she always inspired.

"You know Mr. Ramone?"

He gave a reluctant nod of his head. "For a very long time."

"Did you follow him to London?"

"I did," he admitted.

She sucked in a steadying breath and he could feel the struggle being waged within her heart. She had said that she needed the truth, but Sebastian realized that deep within her she dreaded what that truth might mean.

Perhaps she already suspected that he was not precisely what he pretended to be.

"Did you follow him because you suspected that he was a vampire?" she demanded in commendably steady tones.

"Because I knew that he was dangerous and needed to be watched," Sebastian hedged.

She tested his vague words, clearly not satisfied with his brief explanation.

"Is that what you do? Hunt vampires?"

He swallowed a rather hollow urge to laugh at her absurd accusation. Whatever her lovely sense of wit, he was quite certain that she would fail to find the humor in the situation.

"Not at all," he assured her. "As I said, I am a scholar, nothing more."

"But . . ."

"Amelia," he swiftly broke into her confusion. "Following Mr. Ramone was only part of the reason that I traveled to London."

She stilled, seemingly caught off guard by his

confession. Once again her tongue peeked out to dampen her lips, revealing the unsettled nerves that she was so desperately attempting to disguise.

"What was the other part?"

He took a cautious step closer to her. He wanted to be nearby because of the very real possibility that she might suddenly feel the need to bolt.

"You," he said softly.

Her eyes widened in shock. "Me? Why?"

"I knew that you possessed the amulet."

A gasp echoed through the air as Amelia hastily clutched the amulet about her neck. She did not even seem aware of the protective motion, although Sebastian noted it with a sense of satisfaction. Amelia might not understand the power of the Medallion, but she was clearly not willing to hand it over.

Most reassuring.

"You desire my necklace?" she demanded.

"Be at ease, Amelia." He lifted a comforting hand. "I do not covet the amulet as does Mr. Ramone. My only interest is ensuring that it does not fall into his hands."

She continued to eye him warily, her fingers still tightly gripping the Medallion.

"How could you possibly have known that I possessed the amulet?"

He carefully considered his response. Blast, but he felt as if he were waltzing through a quagmire. One misstep could ruin his tenuous relationship with this woman forever.

"I was told it was given to you."

"By the Gypsy?" She frowned, then gave a pained shake of her head. "No, Mr. Ramone claimed that she was not a Gypsy at all, but a vampire."

The brief but revealing display of her confused vulnerability struck fiercely at Sebastian's heart. Standing there in the thin muslin nightrail with her tousled raven curls, she appeared to be little more than a child. Far too young and fragile to bear the burdens she had been forced to shoulder.

Worst of all, he had no notion of how to make any of this easier to endure.

Not when he was destined to cause her even more grief.

He winced before grudgingly squaring his shoulders. He could avoid the unwelcome revelations no longer.

"Nefri," he said in clipped tones.

"Yes," she agreed slowly. "That was the name that he gave her."

"She is the most powerful and wise of all vampires."

A shadow drifted over her face as she absorbed the significance of his confirmation of what must seem to her a figment of her worst nightmares.

"How . . . how do you know that?" Her gaze frantically searched his features, perhaps desperate to reassure herself that he had not changed into a monster before her eyes. "Sebastian?"

"You are certain that you desire the truth?"

She bit her lip until she drew blood, but with that stubborn courage that he so admired, she kept her gaze steadily locked with his own.

"I must know."

Sebastian heaved a sigh, his hands clenching at his side. Bloody hell. He wished that Lucien, or even Gideon, were here. They were both far more experienced in handling the peculiar emotions of mortal maidens. No doubt they had easily managed the women they had been commanded to protect with perfect ease. He, on the other hand, was far more comfortable hiding behind one of his books. He was bound to make a botch of this.

Pushing back the heavy strands of his hair, he heaved an unwitting sigh.

"It was Nefri who sent me to London. She wanted me to protect the amulet, as well as you, from Mr. Ramone."

"I . . ."

She was shaking her head in denial even before he finished speaking. Her expression was nearly undoing Sebastian.

It was more than fear, or even dread. There was a poignant ache of disappointment that he did not believe he could endure.

"Amelia." He instinctively stepped forward, only to halt when she hurriedly backed from him.

"Why would she send you?" she demanded, still unwittingly clutching the Medallion as if she could gain courage from it.

"Because I was chosen by the Great Council of Vampires to come."

"No." Without warning, she sank to her knees, her head bowed so that her hair tumbled forward to hide her face. "No."

Moving swiftly, Sebastian was kneeling at her side, his arm gently cradling her shoulders.

"Please look at me, Amelia."

He heard her choke back a sob of distress. "A vampire. Dear God."

Sebastian was out of his depth and utterly uncertain as to how to comfort the poor maiden. Silently he cursed Nefri for thrusting Amelia into such danger, and himself for not having the skills that were clearly needed.

"Amelia, you must not fear me," he murmured, pressing his lips to the soft satin of her hair. "I would never harm you."

She shivered, but much to his relief she slowly lifted her head to meet his anxious gaze.

"I do not fear you, Sebastian," she said softly. "As ridiculous as it might be, I somehow know you would not hurt me."

He released a shuddering breath, his hand moving of its own accord to cup her pale cheek. She had not fled, nor fallen into hysterics. She had not even condemned him as a villain. Instead she had willingly listened to the whispers of her heart, rather than giving in to panic.

Her astonishing valor never failed to amaze him.

"It is not at all ridiculous," he assured her. "It is the bonding."

Not surprisingly, her brows drew together in bewilderment. "The what?"

"The bonding." His thumb shifted to absently stroke the corner of her mouth. Inanely he recalled just how sweet those lips had tasted. How they had tempted him to drown in their promised pleasure. "It gives one the power to sense and feel what is within the soul of another."

She merely gazed at him for a long moment. "Oh."

"What is it, my dear?"

"This is all so bewildering," she whispered at last, closing her eyes as if wanting to shut out the vast upheavals that had tortured her so this evening. "Heavens above, I did not even believe that vampires existed just a few hours ago. Now I learn I am being hunted by one and protected by another."

Pulling back, Sebastian regarded her pale features. Even in the shadows, he could not miss the lines of brittle strain. His heart clenched. Brave or not, Amelia was near to total collapse.

Unfortunately, the stubborn woman would never

admit to such a weakness. It would be up to him to insist that she have a care for herself.

"You are tired, my dear. I will take you to your chambers and then escort William to his own. We will speak of this further on the morrow."

"Yes," she agreed wearily, allowing Sebastian to tenderly pull her to her feet. Only when he reached down to firmly scoop her into his arms did she seem to come out of her fog of bewilderment. "Sebastian?"

He smiled deep into her eyes as he smoothly moved out of the library and toward the stairs.

"For once allow someone else to care for you, my dear," he commanded softly. "You do not have to be strong tonight."

To her utter astonishment, Amelia discovered herself tumbling deep into sleep the moment her head was laid upon the pillow.

Whether it had been the stress of the night, or the soul-deep knowledge that she was safe within Sebastian's home, was impossible to say. All she did know for certain was that when she awoke to discover the late morning sunlight shafting through the chamber, she felt considerably stronger.

Rising into a seated position, she gazed about the room Sebastian had carried her to only a few hours before. It was nicely situated with a bay window overlooking the front street. The furnishings were typically English with yellow satin wall panels adding a lovely brightness. But as with most of the house, there was a decided air of neglect.

With the careful eye of a woman already in control of her own household, she took disapproving note of the dust clinging to the tall armoire and the dullness of the mahogany chairs and tables. It was only when she was debating the effort of polishing the delicate crystal chandelier overhead that she at last realized the absurdity of her thoughts.

What did she care if the entire house could use a good scrubbing? Or that there was a dampness in the air? Such things were meaningless nuisances that she was using to hide her true troubled thoughts.

Perhaps not surprising, she acknowledged wryly.

Who would not prefer to dwell upon spider webs and dust rather than face the brutal truth that her entire world had been thrust upside down?

Unwittingly she clutched the blankets up to her chin. Vampires. Was it even possible? Until yesterday she would have thought anyone mad to claim that such monsters existed, let alone walked the streets of London. But, on the other hand, how could she deny what she had witnessed?

She had seen Mr. Ramone with blood shimmering on his lips. She had seen him shift into nothing more than shadows before her very eyes.

And there was that . . . tingling awareness within herself that she could no longer deny.

Her fingers lightly touched the Medallion about her neck. Whatever the powers of the amulet, she feared that they were affecting her. Perhaps even altering her. She could see the world more clearly, her senses heightened to an aching sensitivity. It was in the heavy warmth of the air, the faint scratch of the linen sheets against her skin, and the scent of dust and old wax.

More astonishing, if she were to close her eyes she knew she would be capable of knowing the precise location of Sebastian, and, to a lesser extent, her brother. She even feared she might be able to sense the distant presence of Mr. Ramone.

As if to prove her point, a sudden rash of goose bumps tightened her skin. Turning her head, she watched as the door to her chamber was opened and Sebastian stepped in.

Beneath the cover, her body trembled. Not from fear. As she had admitted last night, she could not bring herself to believe this man would harm her. No matter what he was. But that did not stop the stark realization that he was not the person she had presumed him to be.

He was mysterious, dangerous, and intent upon fulfulling his duties. Duties that she must force herself to acknowledge were far more important than her or her happiness.

The silver gaze was guarded as he studied her sleep-flushed face. Then, with slow steps, he crossed to settle upon the edge of the mattress.

Amelia was immediately conscious of his male heat. Vampire or not, he was still compellingly beautiful, his burnished hair framing the pale, finely chiseled features and his muscular body attired in a golden coat and ivory breeches.

And he still managed to send a thrill of sensuous awareness searing through her blood.

Warily she forced herself to meet the piercing gaze, futilely hoping that he couldn't read the wicked direction of her thoughts.

"Good morning, Sebastian," she managed to croak.

"Amelia." He continued to search her countenance, as if seeking reassurance that she was not about to plummet into hysterics. "How are you this morning?"

She suppressed an absurd desire to laugh. How was she?

Confused, terrified, and wishing that she could convince herself that this was all some horrible nightmare.

She clutched the covers closer to her chin. "I am well. Have you seen William?"

"Yes. He is eating his breakfast in the kitchen."

"Oh." It took a moment before her brows abruptly drew together and the terrible memory struck at her heart. "But your housekeeper . . ."

The elegant features hardened with a dangerous anger before he began to ease the tension from his body. It was not gone. Amelia could still feel the frustrated heat smoldering, but it was more under control.

"Thankfully I am capable of producing a passable meal when called upon." He gave a faint grimace. "Well, perhaps *passable* is a rather generous choice of words, but it is edible."

With a faint pang, Amelia realized that she had not even considered Sebastian's own loss. He would no doubt blame himself for the death of his servant.

"Thank you for caring for William," she said softly.

" 'Tis nothing, my dear."

"It is far more than most gentlemen would do," she uttered unthinkingly before abruptly blushing in confusion.

Swiftly realizing the cause of her discomfort, Sebastian offered her a wry smile.

"I may be a vampire, Amelia, but I also hope that I am a gentleman."

Her blush only deepened at his words. "Of course you are. I am sorry."

Regret, and something that might have been pain, flashed through the silver eyes as he studied her bewildered unease. Reaching out, he lightly touched a curl that lay against her cheek, his touch sending a poignant sweetness through her body.

"Perhaps we should finish our conversation," he murmured.

She bit her lip. A cowardly part of her wanted to close her ears and pretend that none of this was occurring. Perhaps if she ignored it all, it would simply go away.

But the greater part of her rebelled at such foolishness. She had always faced the world as it was, not as she desired it to be. Even this.

"Yes."

His fingers continued to toy with the stray curl, but a distant quality entered the silver eyes, as if he were looking within himself.

"I will not bore you with a long history of vampires, any more than to say that once my brothers roamed freely among humans. Unfortunately, the tales of our savagery were not a myth. A vampire is both blessed and cursed by bloodlust."

She shivered in spite of herself. "Bloodlust?"

"It is a vampire's hunger to consume the warm blood of mortals. By taking the life and soul of a human, we are granted many powers. We possess great strength and are capable of changing our form."

Her breath caught in her throat. She had to distance herself from his words to keep the horror at bay.

"Such as becoming a shadow?" she demanded, anxious to keep talking.

His eyes darkened, easily sensing her raw nerves.

"Precisely. But along with such powers it also brings with it the curse of being vulnerable to both fire and sunlight."

Her brows rose as she noted the pool of light that even now surrounded him.

"Sunlight?"

He smiled faintly. "I speak of the years before Nefri, our leader, created the Veil."

She struggled to follow his peculiar explanation. "What is the Veil?"

"It is a boundary that separates our worlds. Beyond the Veil, vampires are no longer plagued by the hot passions that once ruled us. We live at peace with one another, able to devote our considerable intelligence to elevating ourselves far beyond the brutal predators we once were." Perhaps unconsciously, his features softened as he spoke of his home. She did not need to be told that he deeply felt the loss of being with those of his kind. "The Veil also purified the curse of blood-lust. Unless I were to consume the life of a human, I remain immune."

Amelia attempted to ignore the wistful pang of loneliness that she sensed within Sebastian. It made him seem vulnerable, and almost . . . mortal. And echoed far too closely her own feelings of isolation.

It also threatened to distract her from the troubles at hand.

"But not Mr. Ramone?"

"No." His hand dropped to lie clenched upon the blanket. The mention of his fellow vampire was clearly distressful. "He has chosen to return to a life of violence."

"Why?"

He slowly shook his head, his gaze shifting toward the distant window.

"It is difficult to say. There are always those vampires who believe that it is their right to have dominion over humans. They resent the loss of the powers and their sense of divine superiority."

Amelia regarded him with a frown. It was odd to consider that vampires would be so plagued by human frailties. Pride, conceit, the lust for power.

Whatever their superiority, it did not seem that they had managed to progress far beyond the weaknesses they had hoped to leave behind.

"I still do not understand what this has to do with me."

The piercing gaze returned to her. "The Veil was

created with the powers of an ancient vampire artifact. The Medallion."

Suddenly and sharply, she was aware of the heavy
weight of the necklace as it lay against her skin. The
odd warmth of it spread through her body, bringing
the sense of peace and courage that she had come to
depend upon.

"My amulet?"

"The amulet is but a piece of the Medallion."

She should no doubt have been terrified of the
thought of possessing such a strange and formidable
artifact. Who could possibly know what it was doing
to her? Or how it might affect her in the future?

But she could conjure no unease. The amulet had not
harmed her. Indeed, she had never felt more keenly
aware, more involved with the world about her. She
found it very difficult to imagine a future without its
comforting presence.

Almost as difficult as a future without this gentleman
who had so tangled himself in her heart and soul.

"And it was Nefri who gave it to me?" she demanded.

"Yes, in the guise of an old Gypsy."

"But why?"

He took a moment to consider his words carefully.
Amelia felt a rueful impatience racing through her. He
was a man who always weighed and thoroughly pondered his every thought and action. It was a trait that
she both admired and found oddly frustrating.

Just once, she wanted to see him stripped of his
stark self-control. She wanted to see the truth of his
soul without the carefully constructed barriers that he
hid behind. She wanted him to be as prey to his emotions as she was.

A childish, and perhaps even dangerous, desire, she
was swift to chide herself. She had already seen the

horror of one vampire who readily wallowed in his darker side. Did she truly wish to have Sebastian behave in a similar manner?

"Some time ago it was discovered that three renegade vampires had slipped through the Veil with the intention of gaining command of the Medallion," he answered in careful tones. "Nefri realized the danger should the traitors succeed. She made the decision to divide the Medallion into three amulets and bind them to mortal maidens. As an added precaution, I was sent, along with Lucien and Gideon, to ensure that the amulets were kept safe."

She pressed herself deeper into the pillows, her eyes wide. There were other vampires roaming through the streets of London? And other maidens who were being hunted just as she was?

Her brows drew together at the thought, and then suddenly she regarded him with a question in her eyes.

"Bind the amulets? What does that mean?"

"The amulet is a part of you," he said softly.

She was not unduly shocked. Even now, she could recall the strange warmth that had flowed through her when the Gypsy had pressed the amulet into her hand. She had known then that it was more than a mere piece of metal. The only true mystery was why she had accepted such a dangerous gift.

"I see."

Sebastian leaned forward, his features severely outlined by the sunlight. There was a quiet, relentless strength in that countenance that spoke of a dangerous adversary.

"It was necessary, Amelia," he said, although she was uncertain whom he was attempting to convince. "It was the only way to keep the traitors from merely killing you and taking the Medallion for their own. If you die, the power within the amulet is lost."

"Dear heavens," she breathed, her heart missing an entire beat. "Then why does Mr. Ramone hunt me if it cannot be taken?"

"It cannot be taken but it can be given freely." He regarded her with a solemn expression. "That is what he seeks."

She shuddered as she recalled that dark, glittering gaze as it had regarded the amulet with a savage desire. At least she now comprehended why he had not simply slaughtered her and taken what he so wanted.

The knowledge should have been reassuring, but the thought of Mr. Ramone attempting to lure the amulet from her grasp made her skin crawl.

"Freely given," she muttered. "That is what the Gypsy warned me of."

His hand once again gently cupped her cheek as he regarded her with a fierce expression.

"The amulet must be protected, Amelia. For the sake of both vampires and humans. Should the Veil fall, both our races would suffer unbearably."

Lost in the smoky silver of his gaze, she slowly nodded her head. There was still far too much that she did not comprehend. Questions continued to whirl through her mind. Not the least of which was what Sebastian intended to do with her now. But for the moment she was willing to follow his lead.

"I understand."

His grip tightened upon her cheek. "My dear . . ." His words were abruptly cut off as a sharp knock upon the entrance door echoed through the house. A tight flare of impatience crossed his features before he reluctantly rose to his feet. "I must answer that."

She sat upright, her eyes wide with sudden apprehensiveness. "What if it is the runners?"

"Go to the kitchen and be sure that William is kept

hidden. I will soon rid us of our unwelcome guest," he added, his expression one of dangerous intent.

Amelia swallowed heavily. His even tone helped her to regain control of her ravaged nerves. Nothing could be served by panicking. Unless she did something stupid, no one could possibly know that she and her brother were here.

"Yes."

He regarded her for a long moment before he jerkily leaned forward to press his lips to her own in a startling kiss. It was over in the beat of a heart before he turned and strode smoothly from the room.

Left on her own, Amelia lifted her fingers to touch the lips that still tingled from his brief caress. Then, a faint glow entered her eyes.

Just for a moment, he had not been coolly pondering the best course of action. He had not debated whether he should or should not kiss her. It had been spontaneous and as unexpected for him as it had been for her.

It had been from his heart.

Ten

Once in the foyer, Sebastian paused to smooth his hair. As always, his time with Amelia had left him vulnerable and off balance.

A grudging smile touched his lips. Damn it all, she refused to react in the manner he expected. All of his studies had indicated that she should have been in near-hysterics at this point. Not only to learn that a vampire of legend was stalking her, but that the gentleman whom she had come to trust was a monster as well.

But there had been no tears, no fainting, no panicked flights from his clutches, no recriminations that he had lied and deceived her.

Instead she faced him squarely and demanded the truth without flinching.

It was little wonder he found himself forgetting he was in London only to protect the Medallion.

Of course, a dry voice whispered in the back of his mind, his continuing admiration of her bravery did not fully explain that poignant, utterly impetuous kiss. A kiss he had been as unable to halt as the sun rising in the morning.

Stifling a sigh, he continued across the marble floor. Fair maidens and tantalizing kisses should be the last things on his mind at the moment.

With a flick of his hand he pulled open the door to find a large, bluff-faced gentleman. His eyes swiftly narrowed in caution. Despite the smile on the broad countenance, there was no mistaking the unconscious air of authority that clung to the man's large frame.

There could be no doubt as to the reason the stranger was standing upon his doorstep.

As if sensing Sebastian's wariness, the stranger conjured a self-deprecating smile that was no doubt intended to make him seem a harmless simpleton. A ploy that did not fool Sebastian for a moment.

"May I help you?"

"Mr. St. Ives?"

"Yes."

"Ah." He rubbed his square chin, the smile remaining intact. "I am Mr. Ryan from Bow Street. Forgive me for calling at such an early hour, but I am searching for a young gentleman."

Not without his own skill at deception, Sebastian lifted a cool brow. "Indeed?"

"May I have a moment?" Mr. Ryan ploughed forward despite the obvious rebuff.

"If you wish." With a negligent shrug, Sebastian waved the man into the foyer and then led him to the nearby parlor. For once he was grateful for the dust covers that prohibited any need to offer the man a seat. "I fear my housekeeper is out at the moment."

A shrewd gaze made a quick assessment of the room before returning to study Sebastian's bland expression with a hint of surprise.

"You have no other staff?"

"I am only recently arrived in London and not yet set in my plans. My stay in the city may only be passing."

"Ah."

It was difficult to determine if the man accepted his vague explanation, but Sebastian was little concerned.

If the authorities considered him a suspect rather than William, so much the better.

He planted his hands on his hips in an open display of impatience.

"Now, you said that you search for a young gentleman. Has one gone missing?"

"In a manner of speaking." The runner cleared his throat. "Are you acquainted with Mr. Hadwell?"

"Hadwell?" Sebastian took a moment, as if to consider the name. He was too wily to deny any knowledge at all. It would only convince the man that he had something to hide. "Ah yes. I believe he resides a short distance away with his sister."

Mr. Ryan gave a sharp nod. "Yes. I have a few questions I would like to ask him, but unfortunately he is not at home."

"I fear I have not seen him for some days." Sebastian slowly pleated his brows. "Indeed, I believe I heard my housekeeper mention that Miss Hadwell intended to leave London to visit her parents."

"Ah," Mr. Ryan murmured, his shrewd gaze never wavering from Sebastian's countenance.

"Is that all?"

Mr. Ryan once again cleared his throat in a modest manner. "Actually, I do have a few questions, sir, if you will allow."

Sebastian smiled wryly. He knew quite well that it was a command rather than a request, no matter how cleverly worded.

"Of course."

"First, I fear I must tell you that there has been another murder in the neighborhood."

Sebastian grimaced. He did not need to feign his regret.

"How unfortunate," he murmured. "Did it occur last evening?"

"Yes, not far from here," Mr. Ryan confirmed.
"Could you tell me if you noticed anything was amiss?"

As was his usual custom, Sebastian carefully pondered his answer. His first thought when Mr. Ryan
had so inopportunely arrived had been to send him on
his way with all swiftness. He was far too aware that
one unfortunate noise from his hidden guests could
ruin everything. A risk that was becoming ever greater
as he sensed the presence of Amelia, who was even
now hovering just outside the door.

With an effort, however, he quelled his anxiety.
What was needed now was cool logic. He would
wring Miss Hadwell's lovely neck later.

He searched for some means of using Mr. Ryan's
presence to his own advantage.

"Unfortunately, no. I was home most of the
evening."

"You did not leave the house at all?" Mr. Ryan
persisted.

"Only once, though that was quite late." Sebastian
tilted his head as if attempting to recall the events of
the previous evening. "Indeed, it must have been well
past three. I awoke and was unable to return to sleep
so I stepped out to have a smoke. My housekeeper is
rather a tartar when it comes to a gentleman enjoying
a cheroot, even in his own home."

Although the broad face did not react to the offhand
words, there was no missing the sudden tension that
tightened about the runner.

"Yes, sir. Quite understandable." He rubbed his chin
absently. "Did you happen to notice anyone about?"

"No, I . . ." Sebastian paused deliberately. "Well, I
did happen to see Mr. Ramone pass by. He must have
been in a hurry since he did not appear to hear me
when I called out a greeting."

It was clumsily obvious, but thankfully Mr. Ryan

did not appear suspicious. Instead, his eyes abruptly narrowed in concentration.

"Mr. Ramone? You are certain he was the gentleman you saw?"

Sebastian lifted his brows. "Of course. Even at a distance, his well-pampered curls are unmistakable."

The runner struggled to repress a wry smile. "Quite right."

"I fear I did not notice anyone else about."

"Very good, sir." Mr. Ryan subjected Sebastian to one last searching glance before offering an awkward bow. "I will trouble you no further."

Sebastian graciously escorted the man back into the foyer and opened the door. He was uncertain if he had managed to fool the runner completely, but he could at least be assured that the man's entire attention would not be focused on William.

Stepping onto the front porch, Mr. Ryan paused abruptly and glanced over his shoulder.

"Oh, Mr. St. Ives."

"Yes?"

"If you do come across young William, would you please send word to me at Bow Street?"

He smiled easily. "You may be assured I will not forget."

The runner smiled thinly, perhaps well aware that Sebastian was not being nearly as forthcoming as he would desire. Still, there was little he could do without direct proof.

"Good day, sir."

Turning, the man continued down the stairs and Sebastian firmly closed and locked the heavy door. Only then did he step toward the center of the foyer and cross his arms over his chest.

"All right, Amelia. You may come out," he commanded in exasperated tones. There was a long pause before she stepped slowly from behind a large urn. He heaved a long-suffering sigh. "I thought I told you to wait in the kitchen."

She had the grace to blush, although her eyes flashed with a stubborn fire.

"I had to hear."

"And William?" he prompted.

"He is busily washing the dishes. It is a chore he enjoys."

Sebastian was not at all reassured. The devil take her. What if William had dropped a plate? Or come in search of company?

"It was a risk you should not have taken."

She could not have missed his stern expression and the hint of censure in his words, but astonishingly she moved brashly toward him, the enchanting dimples making a sudden appearance.

"Thank you," she said softly, not halting until she was standing far too close for his peace of mind.

Sebastian struggled to contain his annoyance. Amelia might have ruined all with her impetuous behavior. But even as the thought went through his mind, he already knew it was a lost battle.

How could he possibly remain immune to those dark eyes that shimmered with open admiration, or the sweet smile that made so much pleasure swirl through his body?

He was a vampire, not a bloody saint.

"Thank you for what?" he demanded absently, his mind far more consumed with the sheer muslin that revealed a great deal too much.

"For confusing Mr. Ryan, of course." Seemingly unaware of the sudden prickles of heat in the air, she placed her hands trustingly upon his chest. "You were . . . marvelous."

He did not intend to move, but somehow his hands

found their way to her shoulders. Once there, it was only natural that they would sweep toward the plunging bodice of her nightrail. The warm satin of her skin was like a magnet.

"Hardly marvelous," he was forced to protest, his heart kicking as he felt a shiver race through her body. "I do not believe Mr. Ryan is entirely convinced that you and William have left London."

Her eyes darkened, her hands tentatively smoothing over the muscles of his chest.

"Perhaps not, but now he must consider Mr. Ramone as a suspect," she said, her hands audaciously lowered toward his tightly clenched stomach. "That was quite brilliant."

Sebastian caught his breath, his teeth gritting as her touch sent a violent surge of need through his body. Blessed Nefri. A few more moments and he might forget it was the middle of the morning and they were standing in the center of the open foyer.

It would be so delightfully easy. A few tugs upon the muslin nightrail. A few steps toward the nearby rug. A few kisses. And then . . . paradise.

So much for his notorious restraint, he acknowledged wryly. At the moment he would gladly exchange every book he had ever owned for a soft bed and several hours of delicious privacy with this maiden.

Closing his eyes, he shifted to grasp her roaming hands. The sweet torture was more than any lusty vampire could bear.

"Amelia," he groaned in ragged tones. "You truly are a minx."

Her low chuckle did nothing to ease the aching tension that gripped his body.

"Are you sorry that you were sent to protect me?"

"No." He lifted his lids to gaze deep into her eyes. "No, I am not sorry."

A stillness settled about her as she regarded him with a haunting glimpse of vulnerability.

"Neither am I."

Amelia was on the library floor putting together a simple wooden puzzle with her fretful brother when Sebastian entered the room. Glancing up, she felt her heart skip a beat at the sight of him.

Despite the fact that she had been sheltered beneath his roof for the past two days, she had rarely been allowed to catch sight of him. He claimed that he had been busy ensuring that the devious Mr. Ramone did not make any further attempts to approach her. Perhaps it was a genuine excuse. But she had a deep suspicion that he was deliberately avoiding her company.

Now she found her gaze sweeping avidly over his body and lingering upon the chiseled features that plagued her dreams without mercy.

Her breath caught. The horrifying knowledge that he was not even human should have made his faintly exotic beauty repelling rather than fascinating, and the honey-accented voice something to be feared.

Unaccountably, however, Amelia could not gaze upon him and see a monster to be feared. Nor even a mere guardian who would protect her and then vanish as swiftly as he had arrived.

He was, quite simply, the man who had charged into her lonely world and made her remember that she was a woman.

In silence she watched his approach, sensing the strain that he was careful to keep hidden. She wished she had the power to ease his burdens. Unfortunately, he remained far too aloof for her to offer her comfort.

All she could do at the moment was avoid adding to his concerns.

A faint smile touched his lips as he watched William fiercely concentrating upon the puzzle piece in his tight clutch. Then he slowly turned to meet her searching gaze, the male features seeming to soften at her hint of concern.

"Come." He held out a slender hand. "I have brought you a surprise."

"A surprise?" Amelia readily placed her fingers in his and allowed herself to be pulled to her feet. "What surprise?"

Firmly tugging her arm through his own, Sebastian led her toward the open door.

"Patience, my dear."

She grimaced at his mysterious manner, but in truth she did not mind. It was enough just to be allowed to spend a rare few moments in his company.

Breathing deeply of his warm scent, Amelia shamelessly shifted closer to him as they moved through the hall and down the stairs. She had a dozen questions she wished to ask him, not the least of which was what the demonic Mr. Ramone intended to do next. But her lips remained closed. Her entire body was tingling with the wondrous sense of him. It was too pleasant to distract herself with distasteful thoughts of the treacherous vampire.

In silence, they continued toward the back of the house, and then, pushing open the door to the kitchen, he waved her through.

"What on earth are you up to?" she demanded as she stepped into the narrow room. Only then did she notice the slender woman standing next to the table. Rushing forward, she clutched the work-roughened fingers in her own. "Mrs. Benson," she breathed in pleasure.

"My dear." The servant smiled, although there were

tears in her eyes. "I have been so worried. How is William? Has he been eating properly? Does he have his favorite slippers?"

Amelia chuckled at the flurry of questions. She suddenly realized just how much she had missed the hectic chatter and unwavering love that this woman offered.

"He is quite well," she assured the older woman. "He will be very pleased to see you. I fear I do not make his muffins in the manner that he prefers."

A flush of pleasure touched the wrinkled cheeks as she instinctively glanced about the kitchen with an experienced eye.

"Well, I shall soon have him a batch in the oven."

"You will have ample time later," Sebastian said, firmly interrupting the happy reunion. "First you will wish to settle in your rooms."

"Yes, indeed, that would be lovely," Mrs. Benson was swift to agree.

"There is a sitting room and bedchamber just off the pantry."

Sebastian moved to escort her out of the kitchen, only to be imperiously waved away.

"No, no. I can find them. I shall have a bit of a rest and then see about those muffins. Oh, and there is dinner to consider . . ."

The housekeeper bustled toward the side door, her mumbles following her all the way to her chambers.

Pressing her hands together, Amelia regarded Sebastian with a bright smile.

"Thank you," she said with all sincerity. "I am very relieved to have her with us. I was concerned she might be harmed."

"As was I." He stepped closer, his hand rising to tuck a stray curl behind her ear. Almost absently, his fingers lingered, lightly stroking the sensitive line of her neck. "Unfortunately, your home is being closely watched by Mr. Ryan. I was forced to use a chimney sweep to get word to her that I desired a meeting. It would not have done for me to have been seen upon your doorstep."

Amelia moistened her suddenly dry lips. She wanted to concentrate upon his words. She was certainly interested in how he managed to whisk Mrs. Benson away from danger. Unfortunately, her mind possessed a will of its own. It seemed far more eager to dwell upon the dazzling enjoyment of his touch.

"No, of course not," she at last managed, hoping her expression did not reveal she was a breath away from swooning against him. "How did you manage to bring her here?"

His own thoughts did not appear to be entirely upon their conversation as his gaze followed the distracting path of his fingers.

"I had her walk to her sister's with an obvious bag of belongings. Once there, she slipped out the back and into a hackney I had waiting. It is hoped that all will believe she is set to remain with her sister for some time."

Despite her bemusement, Amelia discovered her more sensible self quite impressed with his ingenious plan.

"You truly are a very clever gentleman."

His lips twisted at her words. "Not clever, merely desperate. I could not bear another day of eating my feeble efforts at cooking."

She gave a sudden chuckle. In truth it would be lovely to have Mrs. Benson's deft hand in the kitchen. The past few days she had existed on eggs and porridge with the occasional slice of ham to break up the monotony. Sebastian was undoubtedly a skilled, intelligent, fascinating vampire. He would never, however, be mistaken for a chef.

"It was not so bad," she hedged with a flash of dimples.

His fingers moved to cup her chin, his expression amused. "What a terrible liar you are, my dear. You should always tell the truth."

Her gaze searched over the male features that were so achingly familiar.

"While you give nothing away. It is very difficult to know what you are thinking."

A fine tension settled in the air between them, a shimmering web that connected them more forcibly than any physical touch.

"No doubt that is for the best," he murmured, his gaze reluctantly lifting to probe deep into her eyes.

"Why?"

He flinched at her question. "Amelia, we both know why."

Of course they did. He was not a London gentleman in search of an on-the-shelf spinster. He was not even a gentleman in the general sense of the word. His only purpose was to ensure that the Medallion was protected. Once he had dealt with Mr. Ramone, he would return to his people and she would be no more than a distant memory.

While she . . . she would be alone again with no one but William to fill her days.

A thought that was far more depressing than it should be.

She lowered her lashes to hide the grief that lanced through her heart.

"Yes," she said softly.

His fingers tightened, all too easily able to sense the pain she sought to keep secret.

"Oh, Amelia, please do not be unhappy," he pleaded.

Knowing that she was only adding to his burdens, she stepped back briskly and tilted her chin to a firm angle.

She did not need his pity. That was the last thing she desired.

"I am not unhappy," she lied bravely, "merely concerned. William and I cannot hide here forever."

Although he could easily read her heart, Sebastian thankfully followed her lead to less dangerous waters. Folding his arms over his chest, he regarded her with a steady gaze.

"It will not be forever. I am certain it will all soon be behind you."

"How can you be so certain?"

"Mr. Ramone . . . Drake, is notoriously vain. His pride will not allow him to remain without the Medallion for long."

She grimaced at his explanation. "That is hardly reassuring, Sebastian."

He smiled wryly, belatedly realizing that his words had hardly been designed to inspire comfort.

"Do not fear. He might very well come to his senses and return to the Veil. If he does not, and continues his pursuit of the Medallion, then I will stop him."

A frown tugged at her brows at his unperturbed tone. "I do not like the thought of you placing yourself in danger."

"No more than I enjoy knowing that you are at risk," he pointed out softly.

"But who will protect you?"

He blinked, as if surprised by her concern. She felt a stab of impatience. For goodness' sake. Surely he must realize that she could not bear it if something happened to him?

"I assure you that I am well able to take care of myself."

She was not about to be so easily soothed. Sebastian had been commanded to protect the Medallion. She did not doubt for a moment that he would sacrifice himself to fulfill that duty.

She settled her hands upon her hips, her expression stern.

"But you said yourself that this Drake possesses powers that you do not have."

"True enough, but I was given a dagger blessed by the most powerful of vampires. If necessary, I will use it to destroy Drake."

His features remained set in determined lines, but Amelia did not miss the sudden darkening of his eyes. For the first time, she considered more than just the danger to Sebastian.

"It would be difficult for you, would it not?" she demanded.

The elegant features tightened. "The most difficult thing I have ever done."

Her expression softened in sympathy. "You were close to this vampire?"

There was a long pause before he shrugged his shoulder. "The relationships between vampires are rather different from those of humans. We are all of one family and connected by more than mere blood. When one of my brothers is lost it leaves a wound that cannot be healed."

"Oh, Sebastian." She closed the small space between them to lay her hand upon his arm. She could physically feel the dread that filled his heart. And the unmistakable sadness at the thought of harming a brother. "Is there no other way?"

He drew in a deep breath. "Who is to say? The future

is not yet established. Not even a vampire is capable of peering into such murky depths."

Amelia sighed, well aware that his hope was fragile, indeed. "I am sorry, Sebastian. I did not realize how very difficult all this must be for you."

A silence descended as he regarded her with an odd expression. "You are a most astonishing maiden, Miss Hadwell," he murmured.

She lifted her brows in confusion. "Astonishing?"

"Most mortals would be mindless with terror at the realization that they were surrounded by vampires. If they were capable of believing it at all."

A most ridiculous blush threatened to rise to her cheeks. She could only wish that she deserved the obvious admiration in the silver eyes.

"To be truthful, this has all happened so swiftly I have not had proper time to think clearly," she admitted with grudging honesty.

His hand gently brushed her face. "You are not even furious you were put at risk by being bonded with the Medallion?"

"How could I be?" She offered an unconsciously wistful smile.

His fingers tightened. "What do you mean?"

"If not for the Medallion, we should never have met."

"Amelia . . ."

Whatever he was about to say was interrupted as Mrs. Benson bustled back into the room, her attention so consumed with her duties that she did not even note the couple who were standing far too close for propriety.

"All right, then, be off with you," she muttered, flapping her hands in their direction. "I can't be making proper muffins with a crowded kitchen."

Amelia sighed.

She could think of any number of things that she desired at this moment.

Unfortunately, muffins were not one of them.

Eleven

Amelia stood at the entrance to her brother's chamber. With her arms folded across her waist, she attempted to appear stern, but she could not prevent her lips from trembling with suppressed amusement.

Tucked in his bed, William had his eyes tightly squeezed shut in an effort to convince her that he was soundly asleep. It was an effort that was bound to fail. Not only did he ruin the effect by frequently opening one eye to determine if she were still there, but he had pulled the heavy blanket up to his chin.

On a night such as this, no one could desire to smother themselves in covers. Thick, stifling heat had choked London for the past two days; long after the sun had set, the unpleasant warmth remained.

She suspected that poor William must be roasting beneath his blanket.

"Already asleep, William?" she asked softly, crossing the room toward the bed.

The eyes squeezed tighter as William clutched the blanket higher.

"Sleeping," he muttered.

"Ah, that is too bad. I had thought perhaps you would like a story before bed."

His nose wrinkled as he considered the delightful

treat. There were few things he preferred more than a thrilling story of knights and dragons before bed.

"Sleeping," he retorted reluctantly.

She moved ever closer to the bed. "Mmm. I suppose I can wait until tomorrow to tell you of Sir William and the magic sword."

One eye popped open. "Magic?"

"Oh, yes. A very, very powerful magical sword. And a fortunate thing, too, since he had to defeat a wicked wizard."

The other eye opened as her brother wavered. "Magic."

"Of course, you probably aren't interested in how Sir William rode upon the black dragon to attack the wizard's tower."

William wiggled, clearly torn between the danger of revealing his secret or missing the story of the brave knight.

At last he heaved a sigh. "No."

Coming to a halt at the edge of the bed, she peered down at his decidedly guilty countenance.

"William, is it not too warm for such a heavy cover?"

He clutched the blanket even tighter. "No."

She swallowed the laughter that bubbled from within. "You are not, perchance, attempting to hide anything from me, are you?"

Realizing his danger, William swiftly squeezed his eyes shut once again. "Sleeping."

"Is there something under those covers, William?"

In response, her brother offered a loud, entirely unconvincing snore.

On this occasion Amelia could not suppress her gurgle of laughter. No one but William could brighten her mood with such ease.

Well, perhaps there was one other, she conceded

ruefully. But since Sebastian had determinedly returned to his habit of careful avoidance, it did not seem to matter. He was little more than a shadow that lurked about the town house.

With an effort, Amelia thrust aside the thought of the elusive gentleman. It was not his fault that she had ridiculously allowed her feelings to become so entangled. Nor that he was destined to leave her heartbroken. He was simply doing what was necessary to protect his people.

At least she would always have William, she staunchly reassured herself. His love would always be with her. Never faltering, never changing. It was a good deal more than many people could claim.

Her smile returned as she gazed down at her brother, who continued to snore loudly. It was time to be done with this amusing charade.

Reaching down, she tugged the blanket loose. William struggled, but it took only a moment before she had the cover off the bed and was meeting his sheepish gaze with a lift of her brows.

"Well, William, what do you have to say for yourself?"

He glanced down at the linen sheet littered with black kittens. "Cats."

"So I see." She cocked her head to one side. "How do you suppose they got into your bed?"

"Cats."

"William." She offered an indulgent smile. She found it difficult to scold him when he looked like a naughty schoolboy. "You know that the kittens belong in their box in the kitchen. It was very kind of Mr. St. Ives to allow them into the house at all. It is not proper for you to take advantage of his generosity."

His lower lip stuck out at the reprimand, but noting

the firmness of her tone, he wisely did not press his luck.

"Bad, William."

"No, not bad," she swiftly corrected, gently replacing the blanket. "The kittens may remain tonight, but first thing in the morning I want them put back in the box where they belong. Is that understood?"

His eyes brightened. "Morning."

"That's right. Now go to sleep." Bending down, she brushed a kiss over his forehead, watching as he snuggled into the mattress with his furry friends.

With a shake of her head, Amelia turned to quietly leave the room. She should perhaps have insisted that William return the kittens to the kitchen immediately, but there seemed little harm in allowing them to remain for one night. It had been difficult enough to keep her brother a virtual prisoner for the past weeks. He should be allowed a few indulgences every now and then.

Closing the door behind her, Amelia turned to make her way down the dark hall. Despite the lateness of the hour, she did not feel weary.

Indeed, an odd sense of restlessness had plagued her throughout the day. It was rather like the feeling before a thunderstorm struck.

Her smile faded as a shiver raced down her spine.

There was something in the air. Something that was raising the hair on her nape and making bumps prickle over her skin.

She unconsciously reached up to touch the amulet that seemed unnaturally warm against her damp skin.

The night promised to be long, indeed.

The screams echoed through the town house, bringing a thin smile to Drake's lips.

Opening the door to the hidden chamber, he regarded the two maidens who were chained to the wall. Most would no doubt be amazed that the ragged, desperate women had only days ago been gracing the most elegant ballrooms in London. The satin gowns were now covered in dust and blood, the arrogant faces marred by stark desperation. In truth they appeared no better than the lowest peasants that littered the stews.

Drake wrinkled his nose at the unpleasant scent that wafted from the chamber.

He had deliberately chosen the two maidens. Not for their beauty, or their charm. After all, a mortal was a mortal. Just another animal. His only interest had been in the fact that they possessed the dark hair and small body that resembled Miss Amelia Hadwell.

A flare of fury raced through his body. There had been a measure of pleasure in torturing the women. It had been quite easy to pretend that the screams that were wrenched from their throats belonged to the galling woman. That their pleas for mercy tumbled from the wench's lips. But the brief satisfaction was no longer enough.

His various ploys to lure Miss Hadwell to his home had come to naught. Because of the Medallion she was impervious to his powers of Compulsion. Furthermore, she refused to be charmed and she would not even be properly cowed.

It was clearly time to use more direct methods.

Tonight he would end this farce.

Moving forward, he halted before the first woman, who sank to her knees in horror.

"Please . . ." she begged, straining against the heavy manacles that bound her wrists. "My father is very wealthy. He will pay you . . ."

With a casual cruelty, Drake grasped a handful of her raven hair and jerked her head backward.

"I have not given you permission to speak, creature," he snarled in disgust.

"No, please . . ."

"Enough." Drake jerked her upward, annoyed with her tears. Mortals were so pathetically weak. "You have served your purpose. Now I fear I have need of your lovely accommodations. I have another maiden who I have awaited for far too long."

The dark eyes widened with fearful hope. "You will release me?"

"Oh, yes. You are about to be released," Drake mocked, his fangs lengthening in anticipation. "Are you prepared?"

The hope remained in her eyes only long enough for her to witness the slow, relentless descent of his head.

"No! No!"

Her scream shuddered through the air as he sank his fangs deep into the firm skin of her neck. Drake fed upon her pain as intensely as he fed upon her blood. The shrill agony fueled his lust, stoking his passions to a fever pitch. All too swiftly, however, her pitiable struggles lessened to mere twitches. He sank his fangs deeper, draining the last of her life.

Her body went limp and he tossed her aside. Slowly turning, he regarded the second captive with a glittering gaze. The woman was moaning, already sunk in fear so deep she was incapable of fighting. He paced to grasp her hair and force her upward. His features hardened with disgust as she continued to moan.

Worthless creature. No courage, no dignity. Simply another maggot that cluttered the streets of London.

Bending his head, he ruthlessly drained her of her life, taking little enjoyment in the kill. Soon, he silently promised himself. Soon he would have

Amelia Hadwell in his clutches. He did not doubt for a moment that she would battle him to the bitter end. A sweet, fulfilling kill made all the sweeter by gaining command of the Medallion.

Tossing the woman aside like a piece of rubbish, Drake produced a snowy linen handkerchief to wipe the blood from his lips. Then, reaching out with his thoughts, he called to the minions who waited above.

Within moments he could hear the uneven scuffle of heavy boots upon the stairs. He moved toward the door as the two burly men entered. Only a few days before, the ruffians had been the undoubted rulers of the underworld. Brash, ill-tempered, with an ugly habit of killing those who opposed them, they had possessed little fear of the elegantly attired gentleman who had strolled into their dingy alley.

They had still been laughing when he had reached out his hand to crush their minds. Now, under the grim grasp of his Compulsion, they no longer laughed. The broad faces were slack, their eyes devoid of intelligence. They would stand in place until death unless he commanded them into motion.

"Take these bodies to the river," he ordered with a wave of his hand toward the dead maidens. "Then return here. We have a very busy night ahead of us."

As if being jerked forward by invisible strings, the two henchmen crossed the cellar to obey his commands. Assured that his scheme was properly set into motion, Drake left the gruesome task to his servants.

He needed to change into something more formal, he decided with a cold smile. Tonight he would gain command of the Medallion, and crown himself the ruler of all vampires. It was only fitting that he appear suitably magnificent.

His soft laugh echoed eerily through the darkness.

***

The heat was unbearable.

Stripped to the waist, Sebastian left the closed confines of his chambers. He was restless. The house slumbered in darkness as he silently prowled through the halls, but there was a hint of disquiet in the thick air. It was that barely discernible unease that made it impossible for him to settle down for the night.

Perhaps he should seek out Drake, he thought as he pushed open the door to the library. If nothing else, he could reassure himself that the treacherous vampire was not plotting anything foul. Of course, that would mean leaving Amelia here alone. His heart gave a squeeze of alarm. No. He would not leave her unprotected. Not on this night.

Stepping into the room showered in silvery moonlight, Sebastian moved toward the center before he came to a sudden halt.

Just for a moment he wondered if his brooding thoughts of Amelia had conjured up her image. If so, they had managed to create a dangerously faultless illusion.

His breath was stolen as he regarded her standing next to the window. The silver light bathed her slender form with a soft glow and shimmered on the long hair that flowed like satin down her back. The flimsy silken gown easily revealed the enticing curves of her body. She might have been a creature of moonbeams. A delicate nymph made of iridescent shadows.

Then the warm, potent scent of her skin assaulted his senses and a shudder raced through him. No, this was no magical nymph, but a full-blooded woman who stirred his passions to a searing pitch.

Sebastian struggled to rein in the hunger that flowed

through his blood. A hunger that was dangerously close to overwhelming his reason.

"Amelia," he called softly.

No doubt already aware of his presence, she slowly turned to face him, her expression troubled.

"Good evening, Sebastian."

Instantly on alert, he moved forward, not stopping until he was a mere breath from her.

"What is the matter, my dear?"

Her gaze rested briefly on his bare chest before reluctantly lifting. "Nothing. I could not sleep, so I thought perhaps a book . . ."

The words trailed away as she moistened her lips in a revealing motion. Sebastian gritted his teeth, feeling the fierce awareness of her own smoldering desire. He should return to his chambers, he sternly warned himself. The heavy pulse of awareness was too potent on this night. It would take one glance, one touch for both of them to be consumed in flames.

But even as he acknowledged the peril, he discovered himself lost in the dark beauty of her eyes.

"Ah."

"I am sorry if I woke you."

"No, I was not asleep."

The small pink tongue once again peeked out to touch the fullness of her lips. Sebastian swallowed a groan.

"It is very warm, is it not?" she demanded in husky tones. "I do not recall a summer in London so smothering before."

If it had been warm before, it was now blazing. A fine sheen of perspiration spread over his skin.

"Yes, it is very warm. Do you dislike the heat?"

"It can be discomforting," she admitted.

His lips curved in wry acknowledgement. "Indeed."

As if realizing he was speaking of more than the temperature in the air, her absurdly long lashes fluttered downward. The hint of confusion was oddly erotic.

"At least William is settled for the night. He was rather restless earlier."

Sebastian sucked in a deep breath. The last thing in the world he desired to discuss was Amelia's brother. Not when she was standing mere inches from his stirring body. Not when the scent of her filled his senses. Not when he had only to lower his head to capture the sweet lips in a kiss that would sweep both of them into paradise.

"I know that it is difficult for him to remain hidden," he followed her lead with an effort. "It is little wonder that he is restless."

"Yes." She paused before wrinkling her nose. "I fear that he sneaked the kittens into his bed. It was very naughty of him and I have made him promise to return them to the kitchen the first thing in the morning. I hope you do not mind?"

"Of course not." He regarded her pale complexion for a long moment. "You are very patient with him."

She lifted her gaze in surprise at his words. "He is my brother. And I love him."

"You speak of it so casually, but such devotion is rare. I can think of no other maiden that I have ever encountered who would willingly surrender her own needs to ensure the happiness of another."

A hint of color touched her cheeks. "That is absurd."

"Is it? Tell me how many of your acquaintances are struggling to provide a home for their family rather than fluttering their way through the Season?"

The blush only deepened. "Sebastian."

Sebastian offered a slow smile. She would never admit that she had done anything extraordinary in saving her brother from the asylum.

"Very well." His gaze shifted on its own to the

provocative shimmer of her pale skin. The brief distraction had done nothing to ease the tension that throbbed between them. "I will leave you to find your book."

He had every intention of turning to leave, but even as he sternly commanded his reluctant feet to move, she was reaching up to lay her hands softly upon the bare skin of his chest.

"No. I . . . I do not wish to be alone."

Sebastian froze, his throat closing as he battled the dark lust that flared through him. Not now, he fiercely warned his surging passions. Amelia was clearly troubled. She needed his strength, not his aching desire.

Lifting his hands, he covered her fingers as they lay against him.

"What is it, Amelia?"

A frown tugged at her brows. "I do not know. It is ridiculous, but I cannot be at ease. There is something in the air that troubles me."

Sebastian felt a measure of surprise. How could she possibly sense the vague threat that had plagued him throughout the day? Unless . . . his gaze lowered to where the Medallion lay against her skin.

"I will remain if you wish," he said in low tones.

"Thank you."

He regarded the dark, vulnerable eyes, his desire abruptly threaded with deep tenderness.

"Shall I read to you the intriguing philosophies of Plato? Or do you prefer the teachings of Aristotle?" he teased.

A prompt grimace eased her frown. "Neither."

"Philistine," he chided.

"I wish you to tell me of yourself."

He was caught off guard by her sudden demand. "What do you wish to know?"

"Everything."

"Everything?"

The raven curls rippled down her back as she tilted her head upward to meet his bemused gaze.

"Tell me of your life."

He gave a rather wry smile, recalling the endless years that had rolled past with barely a ripple. There had always been a vague contentment in his studies. Even an edge of arrogant satisfaction in his superior existence.

It was not until Amelia had crashed into his life that he realized that there had been something missing in that placid contentment. Now he feared that he was very much addicted to the chaotic passions she had unleashed.

"You would no doubt consider it a tedious existence," he admitted. "I devote most of my hours to various studies and debates with my brethren."

Not surprisingly, she wrinkled her nose in distaste. "There are no entertainments?"

His smile widened. "Our view of entertainment tends to be less frantic than that of humans. We are Immortals, after all, and possess endless opportunities to appreciate a fine work of art or compose the perfect sonata. I have devoted centuries to a single sculpture. Mortals do not enjoy such luxury."

Amelia stiffened at his words, her expression becoming guarded. Belatedly he feared that his words must have reminded her vividly of the differences between them.

"No, I suppose we do not," she murmured.

"Amelia, what is it?"

"You are an Immortal. How insignificant a mere maiden must seem to you."

"No." He squeezed her hands tightly. "Never insignificant."

The dark eyes searched his with a barely concealed

anxiety. "But how could I not be? I shall be here and gone while you continue for an eternity."

Reaching out, he softly cupped her cheek in his hand. Insignificant? The mere thought was enough to make him bite back a choking laugh. She might as well claim that the moon and the sun were insignificant.

"Amelia." He patiently waited for her gaze to lock with his own.

"Yes?"

"As I said, not even vampires can read the future. You are the bearer of the Medallion. It offers you powers far beyond those of other mortals."

Her brow wrinkled in concentration. "Powers such as the binding you spoke of?"

His heart missed a full beat. Now was not the time to speak of such things. Not when the darkness was weaving its potent magic.

"Yes."

Seemingly unaware of the danger kindling in the air, she slowly brushed her fingers over the skin of his chest. Sparks of delicious heat attacked him.

"What does it mean? What will happen to us?"

His thoughts threatened to cloud up as he grimly grasped her fingers and held them still. He knew precisely what was about to happen if she continued to stroke him in such a fashion.

"I think it best that we discuss such things on the morrow," he husked.

"Sebastian." She regarded him steadily, her expression somber. "You have done your best to avoid and distract me. I would far prefer the truth. What has happened between us?"

Twelve

Amelia felt lightheaded as she gazed into the impossible beauty of Sebastian's countenance.

The odd sensation could easily have been blamed upon the unbearable heat. Or the sleepless nights. Or even the disturbing tension that had plagued her throughout the day.

But she knew quite well that none of those could explain her pounding heart and the honey heat that poured through her blood.

It was those eyes, she silently concluded. Those silvery eyes with their eternal wisdom and that calm, gentle strength. Eyes that could hold her heart captive with frightening ease.

And of course, she wryly acknowledged, her sense of dizziness was not notably eased by the wide, naked bulk of his chest. It was little wonder that gentlemen were expected to keep themselves decently covered. If maidens were exposed to the sight of smooth male skin stretched over muscles that rippled with fluid ease, there might very well be a riot throughout the ballrooms of London.

Inanely she recalled the feel of warm silk as her fingers explored the fascinating planes and angles of that chest. An exploration that might have continued far longer if he had not brought such a firm halt to her forbidden pleasure.

Her breath caught and she sternly chastised herself for the treacherous meanderings of her thoughts. Unbridled lust might be a novel and startlingly delicious experience for an innocent maiden, but at least it was a perfectly normal, human emotion. Her concern should be focused upon those sensations that were decidedly foreign.

Sensations no mere mortal should be capable of experiencing.

With an effort she sucked in her breath and regarded her companion's closed expression. Tonight she was determined to have answers to the questions that had plagued her for days.

"Sebastian?" she prompted as the silence stretched.

He grimaced at her expectant expression. "You can be very stubborn."

"Yes."

"And far too persistent."

"Yes."

A reluctant smile twitched at his lips. "Ah, Amelia, what am I to do with you?"

"What is it you desire to do with me?"

Stillness cloaked him at her unwitting words, the silver eyes darkening with a dangerous awareness.

"That is a very intriguing question, my dear."

Amelia did not miss the sudden tension that crackled in the air. Hell's bells, she would have to be dead not to have noticed. It seared over her skin and raced through her blood. Still, she grimly refused to be distracted upon this occasion.

"Sebastian, tell me of the binding," she said in a determined tone.

Just for a moment he hesitated, as if debating whether or not to deny her request; then, with a faint sigh, he loosened his grip on her hands and took a step backward. Amelia instantly felt the loss of his comforting touch.

"It is what I suppose mortals would consider falling in love," he grudgingly explained. "Unlike mortals, however, such love is not mere emotion that may well fade over time. Instead, vampires become a part of one another."

"A part of one another . . ."

Amelia slowly nodded her head. Yes. That was precisely what she felt.

"That is why I sense you even when you are not near? And why I can feel the very beat of your heart?"

His gaze briefly strayed to where her own heart beat a rapid tattoo against her chest.

"That is a part of the bonding."

"Only a part?" she prompted.

The slender fingers rose to thrust through the bronze thickness of his hair. His movement caused the muscles of his chest to bunch and flex in a most fascinating manner. Amelia ruthlessly bit the side of her tongue to keep her thoughts from straying down unwelcome paths.

"When a vampire discovers his true mate they share what is known as the Immortal Kiss," he continued at last. "It is the sharing of blood that creates an unbreakable connection. They become one heart, one soul, one mind."

"Oh, that is beautiful," she murmured softly, oddly not at all disturbed by the thought of such an intimate joining. Perhaps it was because she had already experienced the tentative edges of binding. Or perhaps it was simply the realization that being eternally connected with this gentleman was something to be cherished, not feared. "Is there a vampire that you have shared this Immortal Kiss with?"

His lips twitched. "No. It happens but once and lasts for all eternity."

"Oh." Her brows drew together. "But . . ."

"What?"

Her wistful imaginings were suddenly shadowed by a prosaically human fear. "I am not a vampire. How could I feel such things?"

He paused a long moment, his gaze lowering to the golden amulet that glowed with unnatural light in the dark room.

"I believe that the Medallion has made you far more sensitive than most mortals." His smile was tender. "In truth, I often forget that you are human."

She briefly touched the warm Medallion, her frown remaining intact. Yes, the Medallion had altered her. Perhaps in more ways than she knew. Yet, her concern remained firmly focused upon Sebastian rather than herself.

Whatever happened in the future, she had no regrets for having allowed Sebastian into her heart. It did not matter that he was a vampire, or even that he might very well leave her alone and unable ever to love again. He had opened her heart to the beauty and the wonder of truly joining her soul with another. He had taught her the perilous excitement of passion. What he had given her was a gift beyond price and one she would cherish forever. Or for as long as she had, she wryly amended.

Unfortunately, she feared that Sebastian was not nearly so accepting of the sudden, fierce whirlwind that had drawn them together.

"What will happen?" she asked softly.

The silver gaze moved over her pale features. "What do you mean?"

She stepped closer to him. "What will happen when

you return to the Veil? Will you be able to resume the
life you had before you came to London?"

"No." His expression was somber as he slowly
reached to take her hand. Keeping her gaze firmly
locked with his own, he pressed her hand to the center of his chest. "The Veil protects us from bloodlust,
but not from our own foolishness. You shall be a part
of me no matter where I am."

She felt the beat of his heart beneath her fingers, but
more than that, she felt it deep within her. That steady,
relentless beat that was now a part of her own pulse.

"I am sorry."

He appeared startled by her words. "Why do you
apologize?"

"This binding—it does not please you."

His breath rasped sharply through his teeth. "No,
Amelia. You are mistaken. It pleases me very much."

It pleased him? He certainly had a strange way of
showing it.

"Then why do you avoid me?"

Beneath her fingers she could feel the sudden jerk
of his heart.

"Because I do not trust myself when I am alone
with you, Amelia. Without the Veil, my passions are
. . . difficult to manage."

She was once again forced to remind herself to
breathe. Odd. She had never forgotten to breathe
before she met Sebastian. But then, before Sebastian she had never felt as if she were drowning in a
gentleman's gaze, or battled the urge to rub against
bare male skin.

"Oh. I thought that you must not share my feelings. Or if you did, that you must regret them."

A hint of amusement flashed through his eyes. "I
have attempted to make myself feel regret. I was,

after all, quite content with my peaceful, scholarly existence."

"And did you succeed?"

"Not even for a moment." Gently he lifted her fingers to press them to his warm lips. "I thought I could rationally choose what would bring me contentment. Fate, however, has decided otherwise."

Amelia gave up on her attempts to catch her breath. Instead, she gazed deep into his eyes with a sense of wonderment. She wished she could capture and hold this moment forever.

"Sebastian . . ." Her words froze upon her lips. The giddy delight that filled her was abruptly stabbed with a malevolent sense of impending danger. Her eyes widened as she felt Sebastian stiffen in similar awareness. "What is that?"

"Drake." With blinding speed, Sebastian had reached down to slip the dagger from his high boots.

Amelia lifted her hands to her throat. Just for a moment she had been able to forget about the ruthless killer who stalked her. Now she was brought firmly back to earth and a shudder raced through her.

"He is close."

"Remain here," he commanded as he turned to move toward the door.

She bit her lip as a powerful fear clutched at her stomach. "Sebastian, be careful."

He took only two steps before coming to a reluctant halt. "Bloody hell. It is too late." Spinning toward her, Sebastian pointed toward the heavy desk that dominated the room. "Get over there."

Amelia did not hesitate to obey. The mere thought of facing the bloodthirsty vampire was enough to make her tremble in terror.

As fast as she moved, however, she had barely reached the desk when a bone-deep chill entered the room. With wide eyes she watched Drake Ramone step into the library with slow, deliberate motions.

Almost inanely, she noted the perfect cut of his black coat and ivory breeches. Even his curls had been carefully crimped and brushed toward the thin face.

A perfect gentleman, she grimly acknowledged, unless one looked close enough to perceive the flat deadness of his eyes and the cold cruelty of his mouth.

A cruelty made even worse when a sneering smile curved the thin lips.

"Well, well, Sebastian," he drawled as he deliberately regarded the taller gentleman's bare chest. "It appears that you are not entirely the eunuch that I feared. Of course, I cannot approve of your taste. Mortals are so utterly repulsive to discriminating vampires."

Sebastian's expression remained stoically indifferent to the insult. "What are you doing here, Drake?"

"I wished to speak with Miss Hadwell." Slightly turning, the intruder performed a mocking bow toward the desk. "Good evening, my dear."

Although consumed with a choking fear, Amelia managed to tilt her chin to what she hoped was an imperious angle.

"I have no desire to speak with you."

Lethal fury flashed through the pale eyes before the taunting smile was forcibly returned to his lips.

"What you desire matters little, my dear. I have given you the opportunity to be sensible. Now, I fear I must be more direct."

Her hands instinctively shifted to grasp the amulet about her neck. "I will not give you the Medallion."

"Oh, I believe you will."

Across the room, Sebastian abruptly stepped toward his brother vampire, his expression set in determined lines.

"It will never belong to you, Drake."

"My words are for Miss Hadwell," the intruder snarled, his hands clenched at his side. "And after this evening I doubt your bothersome interference will be welcome."

Sebastian growled from deep in his throat. "I have no patience with your riddles—if you have something to say, then speak plainly."

"Very well." Drake held out a thin, skeleton-like hand. "Miss Hadwell, I desire the Medallion."

Amelia took an instinctive step backward. "No."

"Why do you remain so stubborn? It can mean nothing to you."

"Sebastian has warned me of your plot to destroy the Veil and return vampires to London. I will not allow that to occur."

His gaze narrowed to icy slits. "And you believe you are capable of standing in my way? You are a fool."

Amelia readily concurred. She was a fool. Had she the least amount of sense she would be fleeing from this dangerous madman with all possible speed. Unfortunately, her knees were barely capable of holding her upright, never mind allowing her to move so much as a step.

Instead, she was forced to meet that threatening gaze with as much courage as she could muster.

"You cannot force me to give you the Medallion."

"Ah, but I can," he drawled.

Sebastian once again moved forward, placing himself between Amelia and the threatening vampire. In his hand the dagger glinted with deadly intent.

"Do not take a step, Drake," he warned. "I do not desire to destroy you, but I will do whatever is necessary to protect Amelia."

A harsh, rasping laugh echoed through the room. "I have warned you to remain out of this, Sebastian.

Miss Hadwell will not thank you if some ghastly fate were to befall her beloved brother."

The icy terror that had gripped Amelia was suddenly forgotten at the mention of her brother. Without a thought, she moved around the desk to confront Drake with a frantic expression.

"William? What do you mean?"

Drake lifted his golden brows with a faint smile. "Did I fail to mention that sweet William is now my guest at a rather remote cottage?"

"No," she breathed, her heart squeezing in horror. Not William. She could not bear it.

Easily sensing her rising panic, Sebastian placed a comforting arm about her shoulders.

"Amelia . . . do not."

She barely heard his words. Her attention was grimly focused upon the smiling vampire standing before her.

"What have you done to him?"

Drake lifted an indifferent shoulder. "For the moment he is merely my guest. I cannot promise, however, that he will remain unharmed for long. My servants will soon grow impatient if I do not appear with the Medallion."

The image of William alone and afraid in some remote cabin brought tears to Amelia's eyes. What sort of monster would harm such an innocent soul?

"No . . . please . . ."

"Amelia." Sebastian sternly turned her to meet his steady gaze. "Do not fear. I will retrieve William."

"He will be dead before you even locate the cottage, Sebastian," Drake retorted in icy tones. "The only way to save him is to hand over the Medallion."

Sebastian's hands tightened upon Amelia's shoulders. "Amelia, you must not."

Swallowing the thick lump in her throat, Amelia

squarely met the warning gaze. She fully understood Sebastian's fierce desire to keep the Medallion from the vile traitor. He had to consider what was best for vampires. It was his duty.

She, however, had a duty to William. A duty that she would not deny, no matter how great the cost.

"Sebastian, I will not allow William to be harmed."

His features hardened to forbidding lines. "Drake will kill your brother no matter what you do. And you as well. I will not allow you to do this."

Her heart squeezed with regret, but her resolution never faltered. She loved this gentleman with all her heart and soul, but she could not abandon William. Not for anyone or anything.

"I am sorry, Sebastian, but it is not your decision to make," she said in low tones.

His brows snapped together at the determined expression upon her pale features.

"You will sacrifice yourself, and perhaps all mortals, on the impossible hope that this traitor can be trusted?"

She bit her lip at the harshness in his voice. "I have no choice."

"Amelia, you are being utterly irrational."

Unnervingly aware of Drake's glittering gaze and the ominous chill that shivered over her skin, Amelia reached up to gently touch Sebastian's cheek. She could not hope that he would comprehend, or even forgive, her obligation to William. But she had to at least make the effort to explain her rash behavior.

"Perhaps it is irrational," she admitted in sad tones, "but I will not allow William to be harmed. For his entire life he has been treated as an embarrassment, a mistake that his own family desired to hide away and forget. I am the only one who has ever fought to ensure that he is treated as a person of worth. I will not turn my back upon him now."

Something that might have been pain rippled over his elegant features, but his mouth remained set in a frustrated grimace.

"You are not thinking clearly, my dear."

There was an impatient rustle as Drake shifted closer to Amelia, filling the air with a stench of cold, relentless steel.

"On the contrary, Sebastian," he drawled. "She has at last come to her senses. Now let us be done with this. I will have the Medallion."

Reluctantly turning toward the ghastly intruder, Amelia forced herself to square her shoulders. A frightening plan was beginning to form in her mind. Unfortunately, she was uncertain that she possessed the nerve to carry it through.

She had always considered herself a bold, courageous woman. A woman who faced life and all of its troubles without flinching. Only now did she truly grasp the realization that it was a simple matter to be bold when confronted with meaningless fears. What did the censure of society, or the disappointment of her parents, or even organizing her own household mean when compared to the thought of what must now be done?

Courage without sacrifice was effortless.

"No," she said firmly.

"What?" Drake snapped.

"Not until I can be with William and make sure that you keep your word that he will be allowed to leave."

An ugly frown twisted the too-perfect features. Just for a moment, she feared that his arrogant temper would overcome his desperation for the Medallion. Then, with an obvious effort, he gave a stiff nod of his head.

"Very well. Come."

Sebastian's low groan echoed through the air. "Amelia, no. Do not do this."

She slowly moved closer to him, her eyes filled with remorse. "I am sorry, Sebastian."

His gaze anxiously swept over her, almost as if he were aware of her dark scheme.

"You speak of saving William, and yet you expect me to allow you to walk into danger."

"I . . ."

"Enough," Drake snapped in annoyance. "I weary of waiting for what is mine. Either you join me, Miss Hadwell, or your brother dies."

"Forgive me." Keeping her gaze locked upon Sebastian, she covertly reached to slip the dagger from his fingers, tucking it into the sleeve of her gown before turning toward the impatient Drake. "I am ready."

Reaching out, the vampire grasped her arm and roughly hauled her against him. He was wise enough, however, to keep a wary gaze trained upon the furious Sebastian.

"Do not think to follow," he warned as he deliberately tightened his grip upon Amelia to a punishing level. "Unless you wish to have this delicate flower crushed beyond recognition."

Visibly trembling, Sebastian clenched his hands at his side, the promise of dire retribution smoldering in his silver eyes.

"Drake, I will destroy you if you harm her."

The vampire merely laughed at the threat. "Soon I will possess the Medallion and you, along with all vampires, will be bowing to me."

Sebastian's nose flared with loathing. "It will never be."

"Oh, yes. No one can stop me now." With a sharp jerk, Drake sent Amelia stumbling toward the door. "Prepare to bend your knee to me, Sebastian."

Feeling Sebastian's gaze upon her, Amelia refused to glance backward as she was roughly hustled from the library. She could not afford to witness the disappointment she was certain to see in his eyes. Not now.

William, and perhaps the entire race of vampires, depended upon her to maintain her staunch resolve.

She could not falter.

Her stoic resolve, however, did not prevent the tears from clouding her vision, or the ice-cold fear that was lodged in the pit of her stomach. She had never been so terrified in her entire life. Nor so heart-wrenchingly sad.

She had just discovered the man of her dreams. Now she would never, ever see him again.

Thirteen

The drive through London and into the dark countryside was interminable. Perched stiffly on the edge of the carriage seat, Amelia did her best to ignore the vampire who lounged directly opposite her. Not an easy task when his cold eyes remained locked upon her pale face and the smell of him filled the air.

Somehow she had hoped that once she made the decision to go with Drake, a numb acceptance would protect her. Absurdly, however, as the miles rattled past, the thick, pulsing fear only increased.

With every turn of the wheel she was being hauled ever further from Sebastian. She could physically feel the distance growing between them. Soon enough there would be no more than the faintest sense of him. She was forced to accept the knowledge that she was alone and at the mercy of a murderous, unfeeling monster.

In desperation she blocked out all thoughts of Sebastian. She should be considering William, she sternly reminded herself. The poor boy was no doubt hysterical by now. He was in a strange place with ruffians who had forced him from his bed, and who knew what else. He would be calling for her and unable to understand why she was not at his side.

Her heart gave a sharp twinge. If only she could

save William, then all would be well. That would give
her all the strength she needed.

She kept that thought foremost in her mind as they
continued ever onward. And onward. She barely noticed
the passing fields or the thickening woods about them.
Not even when the carriage at last rolled to a halt.

Indeed, Amelia had barely assimilated the fact that
the sickening sway had come to an end when Drake was
thrusting her out of the door and up a twisting path.

"Move along," the vampire growled.

Struggling to regain her balance, she hurried forward,
her fogged senses briefly discerning a crumbling cottage with a thatched roof. It was just as remote and
desolate as Drake had warned; only the faint glow of
candlelight that could be seen through one of the broken windows assured her that someone was inside.

Reaching the door, she was briefly halted as the
vampire reached out to grasp her arm. Warily, she
turned to study his tight features.

"What is it?"

He paused for a long moment before giving an annoyed shake of his head. "Nothing. Let us be done
with this."

The bony hand reached out to shove the door open.
Amelia did not wait to be pushed forward. Instead,
she rushed into the cramped, dust-shrouded room
with anxious haste.

It took but a moment to spot her brother huddled
in a dark corner. With a soft cry, she moved to kneel
beside him.

"William." She placed her arms gently about his
shoulders, not at all surprised to discover that he was
trembling in fear and weariness. He had probably
been curled in the corner since he had been brutally
kidnapped. "My poor William."

He slowly lifted his head to regard her with wounded eyes. "Bad man."

Tears filled her eyes as she softly brushed his hair. "Yes, they are very bad men."

A growl from behind her had Amelia shifting to face the vampire, who filled the small room with his repulsive presence.

"You see that he is alive," Drake stated in flat tones. "Now give me the Medallion."

Amelia reluctantly rose to her feet, her heart racing so fast she feared it might burst. It had come to the moment of crisis. She would now discover if her desperate ploy would work, or if she had lost all on a daring gamble.

"Not until William is released."

His eyes glittered like shards of glass. "Do not attempt to play me the fool. Sebastian is pathetic enough to be seduced by your wiles, but I am far too clever for such games. If you do not believe me, I can reveal the corpses of any number of beautiful mortals who thought to please my fancy."

She swallowed heavily, not allowing herself to remember the battered and abused bodies of those poor maidens. She had to concentrate upon William. Only William.

"You promised that my brother would be kept safe. I want him allowed to leave before I give you the Medallion."

A dark, nerve-shattering silence descended as he regarded her with malicious fury. The very air seemed to crackle with his fierce desire to punish her for her audacity.

"You try my patience, wench," he rasped, his lengthening fangs suddenly visible.

Amelia nearly balked. Saints above. He was a

ruthless vampire. A beast that killed without mercy. How could she possibly hope to outwit him?

Then from behind her, she heard the faint sound of William's whimper. He had clearly sensed the danger in the air. A danger that only thickened as Drake glared at her with murderous intent. Much to her astonishment, she felt her chin tilting with a renewed determination.

"Do you desire the Medallion or not?"

Her fate hung upon a knife's edge as the pale gaze lowered to the amulet glowing with a tantalizing power. For a heartbeat she was icily aware that his lust to torture her for her daring far outweighed his need for the amulet. Only when her fingers closed protectively over the Medallion did he abruptly regain control of his anger and step back.

"Send him away."

Urging William to his feet, Amelia warily led him across the room, her arms wrapped tightly about him. Once at the door she pulled it open and gazed into her brother's worried eyes.

"Listen to me carefully, William," she said firmly. "I want you to run from here as fast as you can."

His brow wrinkled in puzzlement. "Run?"

"Yes. Run to Mr. St. Ives. He will protect you."

There was a moment of silence before he gave a reluctant nod of understanding. "Run."

"As swiftly as you can."

"Be on with it," Drake interrupted sharply.

Drawing in a deep breath, Amelia shoved her brother with all her strength. "Do not look back, William."

He stumbled, but thankfully he was swift to recover and was racing down the dark path with gratifying speed. Whatever his lack in intellectual prowess, William had always been large and physically strong.

She offered up a silent prayer that Sebastian would rescue her brother before the henchmen who belonged to Drake could find him. She did not doubt for a moment that the stubborn vampire was following as closely as he dared.

Watching as William disappeared into the shadows, Amelia slowly turned back to the impatient Drake. She had done all that she could to protect her brother. Now it was time to pay the cost of that protection.

As if sensing her dark thoughts, the vampire stalked toward her, harsh greed etched upon his face.

"There will be no further delays."

"No," she agreed softly, pulling the dagger from her sleeve. "The time has come."

Drake came to an abrupt halt, but his lips twisted with cruel amusement rather than fear.

"How very charming," he drawled. "Do you think to frighten me with that bauble?"

She grimly lifted the dagger higher. "Do not come any closer."

"Or what?" He deliberately stepped forward. "You will attempt to harm me? Fool. You are no match for my powers. Shall I demonstrate?"

The chill in the room abruptly deepened and to Amelia's shock, the solid form of the vampire began to blur and fade. An ominous fog began to swirl and Amelia was forced to choke back a scream as she realized that the vampire was shifting himself into that strange mist.

It was a bizarre, horrifying spectacle.

"No," she breathed.

An eerily hollow laugh echoed through the cottage. "You are a pathetic animal who only lives because you possess my Medallion. You cannot harm me, Miss Hadwell."

Grasping the last, frayed edges of her courage,

Amelia lifted the dagger and firmly turned it about until the sharp point was painfully pressed to the frantic beat of her heart.

"I have no intention of harming you, Mr. Ramone. I intend to use the dagger upon myself."

Sebastian was aware he was being followed from the moment he entered the thick copse of woods. With fluid motions he slid behind a large tree and allowed the two shuffling men to walk past him.

He did not so much as blink before he was launching himself toward the two and knocking them to the ground. They remained inhumanly silent as he connected a blow to one in the chin and then leaped to his feet to kick the other in the side. Bones crunched beneath his attack but neither hesitated as they awkwardly pushed themselves upright and lunged toward him.

He grimaced at the realization that the men had been caught within Drake's Compulsion. He could already smell the stench of their decay. Nothing short of death would stop them now.

Easily avoiding their outstretched hands, he caught the nearest man about the neck. Holding him before him, he crushed his throat with a sense of regret. The second he dealt with just as easily, allowing the heavy body to drop to the soft ground.

Damn Drake, he silently cursed. The men would have died of starvation within days, or by the hand of the treacherous vampire, but he resented the fact that he had been forced to harm another.

With a shake of his head, he turned from the motionless bodies and sternly turned his thoughts back to the reason he had entered the woods in the first place.

Amelia.

Items purchased at Walgreens may be returned to any of our stores within 30 days of purchase.

Items with a receipt will be exchanged, refunded in cash or credited to your account.

Items without a receipt will be exchanged or refunded by mail within 14 days.

For any return you may be asked for acceptable identification.

I'm Fely. I'm here to serve you with our 7 Service Basics

206   10   7303   00324 030

RFN# 0032-4302-3036-0401-2720

UNISOL 4 12Z   .1A   6.79
    SUBTOTAL   6.79

A 8.25% SALES TAX   .56
    TOTAL   7.35

          CASH   20.00
CHANGE   12.65

OPEN 24 HOURS
THANK YOU
FOR FASTER SERVICE, CALL IN YOUR
PRESCRIPTION ORDER OR PLACE IT ON
WWW.DRUGSTORE.COM 24 HOURS IN ADVANCE

JANUARY 21, 2004   2:46 PM

Not far ahead he could sense her presence. She was still alive, but he was vividly aware of the horrible terror that clutched at her heart. Just as he could sense the reckless fury that filled Drake.

He had to reach her before she did something desperate.

He had barely taken more than a step, however, when there was a loud crashing in the trees ahead of him. Within moments, William came plunging through the overgrowth, his expression wild-eyed and his hair standing on end.

With a low growl of impatience, Sebastian waited for the boy to stumble to a halt before him.

"William."

"Milly," William panted as he reached out to grasp Sebastian's arm. "Bad man."

"Yes, I know, William."

"Milly, Milly," he repeated, shaking in his frustration at not being able to speak of the danger to his beloved sister.

Reining in his the impatience, Sebastian placed his arm about the boy's trembling shoulders. Amelia would expect him to care for her brother with the same tender concern that she would offer. It was now his duty to ensure that the boy was kept safe and secure.

"Amelia will be fine, William. But I must go to her." He firmly lifted William's face to meet his own gaze. "There is a carriage just beyond the trees. I want you to go to it and remain inside. Can you do that?"

He gave a slow nod. "Yes."

"Good lad."

Careful to escort the unnerved young man well away from the bodies lying on the ground, Sebastian pointed William toward the carriage he had left beside the narrow lane. Once he was assured his charge was safely headed in the proper direction, he sharply turned to make his way back through the trees. With the henchmen disposed of, the young man should be quite out of harm's way.

Nearly seething with impatience, he ran through the shadows, his need to reach Amelia so overwhelming that he barely noted the familiar tingles that rushed over his skin. He did not desire to be delayed yet again. Not when he could sense Amelia's dread shuddering through his body.

Unfortunately, Nefri was not a vampire to be ignored, no matter what the urgency. Stepping directly in his path, she held up a slender hand that brought him to a sharp halt.

"Sebastian," she murmured.

Unable to do otherwise, Sebastian glared at the slim figure still attired in her ridiculous rag skirt and full-cut blouse. She appeared more a poor Gypsy than a powerful vampire. No Gypsy, however, could possibly have placed such a forbidding weave about his body. One that ensured he could not bolt past as he longed to do.

"Nefri, I must go. Drake holds Amelia captive."

Her gentle smile was edged with sadness. "Yes, I know. Although I do not believe she is precisely being held against her will."

"She went with him willingly," he grudgingly conceded. "To save her brother."

"Ah." Nefri tilted her head to one side, her eyes glittering in the darkness. "Will she give him the Medallion?"

He flinched, the fierce pain he had been attempting to keep at bay slicing through his heart. He had suspected what she intended from the moment he had watched Amelia leave the room. Even without being able to read her thoughts, her dark sadness had been etched deep within her heart. But he had not allowed himself to ponder the horrible realization. Now, more than ever, he needed his wits clear and unclouded.

"No." He swallowed through the thickness in his throat. "Now that William has been rescued, she will sacrifice herself to keep the Medallion from Drake's hands."

Nefri did not appear shocked. Instead she nodded slowly. "Yes. She is a woman accustomed to giving of herself for others."

Sebastian struggled against the unseen powers. Amelia had given enough. He would allow no more.

"I must go to her," he gritted.

"But, you said yourself that she will protect the Medallion."

"No," His hands clenched at his side, his blood rushing with furious passion. "I will not tolerate any harm coming to Amelia. Not even for the Veil."

Nefri moved through the shadows, her expression one of intrigue rather than anger.

"What are you saying, Sebastian? Surely the life of a mere mortal is not worth the risk of losing the Medallion?"

Not worth the risk? Until he had encountered Amelia he would have gladly agreed with such a callous notion. How could any one soul become more important than the benefit of all? It was simply not logical.

Now he realized that he would sacrifice everything to make sure she was saved from the brutal Drake.

Everything.

"She is not a mere mortal," he informed the ancient vampire in harsh tones. "She possesses more courage and devotion than most vampires, who claim to be so superior. If anyone is to be sacrificed it will be me."

There was a long silence before Nefri astonishingly bowed toward him in obvious respect.

"Go to her then, Sebastian. And be on your guard."

He did not even bother to respond as he felt the barrier abruptly vanish. With sinuous speed he was moving through the trees, inwardly willing Amelia to hold on just a few more moments. He would reach her, he muttered over and over. He would not fail.

Branches tugged at his coat, a handful even scraping against his face as he ducked and dodged through the last fringe of trees. He felt none of them. His attention had narrowed upon the crumbling cottage that at long last came into view.

Slowing to a more cautious pace, he advanced over the overgrown garden, clearly able to hear Drake's rasping voice Drake through the open door.

"Do not be a fool. Simply give me the Medallion and you will be free to join your brother."

"I do not believe you," Amelia responded, an unmistakable quaver in her voice.

"Your brother is still not safe. Even now my servants hold him captive."

"No," Amelia denied. "He is with Sebastian. I have felt them together."

Drake's growl of wrath made the hair on Sebastian's nape rise in warning. The vampire was swiftly being consumed by the bloodlust that pulsed through his body. Soon even his need for the Medallion would be overwhelmed. He would halt at nothing to destroy the young woman who had stood in his path.

"Give it to me," Drake snarled, even as Sebastian gathered himself and charged through the door with a blinding burst of speed.

There was a startled scream from Amelia at his abrupt entrance, but Sebastian could not risk glancing in her direction. Instead he grimly turned toward the silvery mist that hovered in the center of the room.

"Drake."

There was a hiss of fury as the vampire shimmered and at last resumed his mortal form. Stepping forward, he regarded Sebastian with a lethal anger.

"Ah, so the logical, ever-intellectual Sebastian has risked all to save his lover," he taunted.

Sebastian regarded him steadily. The fear that had besieged him that he would not arrive in time was now hardening into a bleak, relentless determination.

"It is over, Drake," he warned.

The thin lips curled into a sneer. "No, you have just allowed me the opportunity to retrieve William. Soon Miss Hadwell will regret her resistance."

So that was why he had not struck out the moment he had entered, Sebastian wryly acknowledged. He still thought to coerce the Medallion from Amelia.

"I fear that William is currently in the care of Nefri."

The pale eyes widened in horror. "No."

"You are welcome to see for yourself," he retorted, taking a step forward.

"Damn you," Drake cursed hoarsely, an odd fear suddenly twisting his countenance. "The Medallion is mine."

In spite of his burning desire for revenge, Sebastian discovered himself regretting the madness that had seized his brother. His brows drew together as he held out a slender hand.

"It is not too late, Drake. Return to the Veil and all will be forgiven."

The vampire briefly regarded the hand, almost as if longing to reach out and join with Sebastian. Then, just when Sebastian allowed himself a measure of hope, he sharply stepped backward with a snarl.

"Forgiven? I will be destroyed if I fail."

Sebastian tensed, recalling the mysterious shadow that had attacked him in the abandoned stables. He still had no notion of who the powerful vampire had been. Or how he had been connected to Drake. But he suspected that Drake deeply feared the attacker.

"Destroyed by whom?" he demanded.

Drake clenched his hands, a reckless glitter in his eyes. "Nefri cannot guard William forever," he said thickly. "I will return and when I do, you will both pay."

Alerted by his warning, Sebastian rushed forward, but as quickly as he moved, Drake was quicker. Shifting his form to a large, black dog, he was bounding past Sebastian and through the door.

Sebastian muttered a curse. He knew he could not allow Drake to escape. The vampire was dangerously desperate and willing to commit any atrocity to achieve his goals. Bloody hell.

Turning toward Amelia, he regarded her with a searching gaze. She was understandably pale with a tense, fragile air about her. The soft curls had tumbled about her shoulders and there were lingering shadows in her dark eyes. His attention, however, was caught and held by the unmistakable drop of blood that glistened against the white skin of her bosom. Directly over her heart.

Blessed Nefri. He had come so close to losing her. Too close. He had to bring an end to Drake, one way or another. He could not take such a ghastly risk ever again.

Moving forward, he briefly gathered her into his arms, squeezing her tightly. With gratifying readiness, she melted into him, her head burying in his shoulder as she allowed the tears that she had been bravely holding in check to be released in choking sobs.

For an endless moment he merely held her close. He needed to have her near. To assure himself that she

was well despite the horror that she had endured.
More than anything, he desired to enfold her in his
own strength.

Slowly she struggled to regain command of herself.
As she did so, she also became aware of the burning
necessity coiled deep within him. It was impossible to
hide from the maiden who had become so much a part
of him.

Leaning back, she regarded him with a worried
gaze. "Sebastian?"

He gently cupped her damp cheek, knowing that the
stubborn minx was bound to try and prevent his determined pursuit of Drake.

"Amelia, you must give me the dagger."

Her face whitened. "Why?"

"We both know this must end tonight," he said softly.
"You and William will be in danger until Drake has
been stopped."

She moaned as she stepped back, clutching the
dagger in a white-knuckled grip.

"I do not wish you to risk your life, Sebastian.
There must be another way."

Sebastian choked back an incredulous chuckle. The
woman had willing allowed herself to be abducted
by a crazed vampire and hauled to this remote cottage.
She had then proceeded to place a dagger to her heart
with every intention of ending her life. And she dared
stare at him with that wounded expression and speak
of risk.

"Bloody hell, Amelia, you are the last person to lec-
ture me about risk."

She refused to reveal even a hint of remorse for the
terror she had put him through. Instead she continued
to regard him with that steady, anxious gaze.

"I could not bear to lose you, Sebastian. Anything
but that."

A fierce tenderness filled his heart at her simple honesty. Once again, he reached out to press her close to his body, breathing deeply of her sweet scent.

"You will not lose me, Amelia. I intend to devote an eternity to loving you."

She tilted back her head to offer him a tearful smile. "Only an eternity?"

"Oh, my love." He pressed his lips to her tumbled curls. He would have given anything to remain holding her in his arms for the rest of his days. Unfortunately, his ability to sense Drake was becoming ever fainter. He had to act swiftly or he might lose him. He pressed a last, lingering kiss to her brow. "Later, my sweet. For now I need you to come with me."

Allowing herself to be held next to his side, Amelia glanced upward as he escorted her firmly toward the door.

"Where are you taking me?"

"Nefri is just beyond the trees, with William. I want you to remain with her until I return."

They had left the cottage and started across the overgrown garden when Amelia came to an abrupt halt.

"Wait."

Sebastian glanced down in suppressed impatience. He wanted his confrontation with Drake over and done with. Only then could he concentrate on his future with this woman he loved with his entire being.

"What is it, Amelia?"

"I do not want you to leave until we have fully become one."

He frowned, wondering if her recent fright had somehow softened her wits. Surely she could not be asking . . .

"What do you mean?"

"You said that we were not yet fully bound. I want to complete the binding."

He was shaking his head in denial before she ever finished speaking. "No, Amelia, you do not know what you ask. It is not a simple ceremony with pretty words as mortals use to join themselves together. The Immortal Kiss means that we are truly bound. Our thoughts, our hearts, our souls. There is no going back. No end. It is irrevocable."

That stubborn expression that he was already learning to rue settled upon her tear-streaked countenance.

"My love is already irrevocable," she said in fierce tones. "All I ask is that we complete our joining."

Sebastian shivered, his heart wrenching with the need to concede to her request. Blessed Nefri. There was nothing he desired more than to make this woman his eternal mate. To have her so much a part of him that it would be impossible to determine where one began and the other ended. But the price was much higher than Amelia could ever suspect.

"Amelia, I fully intend to make you my bride," he said softly, his hand reaching to stroke her cheek. "But not until I have finished with Drake. Until then, it is too dangerous."

Her brows furrowed at his words. "What do you mean, dangerous?"

He grimaced, not wishing to add to her fear, but knowing that he had to be honest.

"The Immortal Kiss would mean that you would be bound to me regardless of what happens this evening. If Drake were to injure me, you would feel my injuries as if they were your own. And if I were to die . . . you would spend an eternity blackened by a grief that would never lessen, never heal."

She bit her lip at his brutal explanation, but her

expression never wavered. Lifting her hand, she pressed it to his heart.

"Such a fate awaits me regardless, Sebastian. If you leave me, my heart will mourn your loss for as long as I draw breath." An unashamed need glowed in her lovely eyes. "Please, Sebastian. Make us one."

Not even a logical, always sensible, scholar could possibly remain immune to the soft plea in her voice, he acknowledged ruefully. And a vampire consumed by love did not have a prayer of denying her request.

There was a brief, futile struggle as his common sense attempted to remind him of all the reasons he should not allow himself to weaken. Then he heaved a small sigh.

He could not battle her desire as well as his own. Not when he was still weakened by the acute fear he'd felt when he'd been so close to losing her.

"Amelia, there is no going back," he felt compelled to warn again.

She smiled with a sweetness that reached his very soul. "That is precisely what I desire."

With a low groan, Sebastian at last loosened the restraints upon his most primal instincts. This was his true mate. The woman who would complete him.

His fangs lengthened in the shadowy moonlight, but Amelia showed no fear. Instead she regarded him with an unwavering trust that did not falter even when he lowered his head toward her. In the silence he could hear the rapid rasp of his own breath and he was forced to pause a moment to gather his nerves. He had to be absolutely in control to avoid causing her any pain.

At last convinced that he was once again in command of himself, Sebastian closed the remaining space to the willing curve of her neck and gently eased his fangs to the satin skin. Within moments, the faintest trace of her blood was flowing through his body, nearly sending him to his knees with the burst of intimatacy that filled his heart.

It was all there. The magical sweetness of her heart, the utter loyalty of her soul, and the overall golden glow of her love for him. It all rushed through him so swiftly that he reeled slightly before pulling back to regard her in amazement. Truly she was a most remarkable woman. And now she was his. Thoroughly and completely.

Lifting his arm toward his teeth Sebastian prepared to complete the binding. He held her wide gaze with his own as he drew blood from his wrist, and then, scooping a drop onto his finger, he pressed it gently to her lips.

Her reaction was just as startled as his own had been.

A small gasp echoed through the silent forest as she clutched at his arms to steady herself. Sebastian swept his arms about her, briefly concerned that the joining had been too powerful for her to bear. After all, she was a mortal despite the Medallion that hung about her neck.

Slowly becoming accustomed to the potent awareness that they were now bound together, Amelia regarded him with eyes that glittered in the moonlight.

"Oh."

"Are you well, my dear?" he asked in concern.

"Well?" Without warning, she tipped back her head to laugh with an unrestrained joy. "Mr. St. Ives, you have just made me the happiest, luckiest, most satisfied maiden in all the world."

Fourteen

It was only with a heroic effort that Amelia allowed Sebastian to leave her in the protection of Nefri as he went in search of the renegade. Sensibly, she understood the need to halt Drake. As long as he remained at liberty he would pose a constant threat to her as well as to William. Even to Sebastian.

Still, such common sense did not keep her from pacing uneasily beside the carriage where William slept. Nor halt the growing sense of dread that was filling her heart.

She knew all too well just how dangerous the treacherous Drake would be when he was cornered. During the ghastly time in the cottage she had sensed his ferocious lust for power. But more than that, she had sensed a deeper, darker emotion. One of fear.

Her brows furrowed as she continued to pace. Why would the vampire so fear failure? Because of the retribution his brother vampires would offer? Surely that could not be the explanation. Sebastian had offered to allow him to return to the Veil in safety more than once. So what was it?

What could force the vampire to risk utter destruction rather than concede that the Medallion was out of his reach?

The bothersome question nagged at the edge of her mind until she sternly reined in her thoughts.

What did it matter? Soon Sebastian would have him trapped and he would be forced back to the Veil or destroyed. Either way, the ghastly threat that he posed would be at an end.

Closing her eyes, she allowed herself to concentrate upon the gentleman who was now a part of her very essence.

He was moving ever further away but she could easily assure herself that he was unharmed and filled with a grim determination. A faint smile chased away her fears. Even at such a distance, she could feel the golden warmth of his love flowing through her.

Unwittingly, her fingers rose to her lips. They still tingled from the fierce, possessive kiss he had bestowed upon her before leaving. A kiss that promised that the intimacy of their joining was far from complete. And that he would very soon tutor her in the pleasures of a more physical nature.

"Amelia."

The soft call of Nefri's voice had Amelia abruptly wrenching her eyes open. An absurd blush stole to her cheeks as she wondered if the wise old vampire was capable of reading her wicked thoughts.

"Yes?"

"Move into the carriage."

Any hint of embarrassment faded as a chill inched down her spine. "Is something the matter?"

The seemingly frail woman lifted her face toward the moon, closing her eyes as if concentrating upon the shadows that surrounded them.

"I feel . . . a strangeness in the air."

Amelia frowned. With great reluctance she turned her thoughts from the wondrous thoughts of Sebastian and concentrated on the velvet darkness that surrounded them. For long moments she could feel nothing but the tingling presence of Nefri. It was a growingly familiar prickle that she knew belonged solely to vampires. But determinedly searching with her thoughts, she at last managed to catch the faint hint of wrongness that had alerted Nefri.

"What is it?" she breathed in puzzlement.

Nefri slowly lowered her head, turning to regard Amelia with a closed expression. "Something approaches."

"Drake?"

"No. This is a force that is much more powerful. And it nears." The wrinkled countenance hardened. "Join your brother in the carriage, Amelia."

With stumbling steps, Amelia rushed to obey the urgent command. The air was beginning to thicken with a bleak dread that was making her skin crawl and her throat tighten. Whatever was nearing, she was quite certain she did not wish to face it.

She had barely managed to wrench open the door and trip up the stairs when what felt like striking lightning hit her in the back and knocked her forward. Gasping, Amelia awkwardly turned to peer out the still-open door.

"Nefri," she breathed in horror, watching the fragile old woman struggling back to her feet as a layer of black shadows shifted and hardened to form a tall, gaunt-faced gentleman.

Valkier regarded the elderly vampire as she scrambled back to her feet. A rare, chilling smile touched his lips. After centuries of plotting and scheming, it was all about to come to fruition. Soon he would be done with this noble, self-sacrificing, aggravating woman. At last she would be destroyed and along with her, the power that she wielded. He alone would be in control of the vampires. And the world.

"Good evening, Nefri," he murmured with an elegant bow.

"Valkier." Her expression hardened as she deliberately allowed the facade of the harmless Gypsy to fade. With a shimmer she was once again a tall, strikingly beautiful vampire with thick, ebony hair that flowed well past her slender waist. The porcelain features were perfect and unmarred by age, although there was no way to disguise the ancient wisdom that filled the ebony-black eyes. "I have been expecting you."

Valkier briefly felt his empty heart flare with the bittersweet emotions that he had once harbored toward this female. An eternity before, he had allowed himself to be held captive by Nefri's beauty. He had offered his very soul to possess her, but the treacherous vampire had denied his attempts at binding. She claimed that her life would be devoted to all vampires. And that she would willingly waste her superior powers in an effort to lure his brothers from their rightful place in the world to imprison them within a Veil.

Now he ruthlessly crushed the unwelcome weakness. Nefri had chosen to oppose him. She would be destroyed for her foolishness.

"How very pleasant to realize that you have not lost your wits entirely, Nefri," he mocked as he stepped toward the beautiful vampire. "I was beginning to fear that you would never realize that I was playing you for a fool."

"No, not a fool. However, I will admit that I hoped that I was mistaken, Valkier." The dark eyes held an annoying hint of sadness. "Despite our differences I have never considered you my enemy. Indeed, I continued to hold the belief that you would overcome

your conceit and realize that our powers are not meant
to compel others to our will."

"My conceit?" Valkier gave a sharp, unamused laugh.
"You have bullied, cajoled, and castrated vampires until
they are no more than pathetic shadows of themselves.
And for what? To cower behind the Veil and pretend
that we do not long to return to our rightful inheritance?
It is your conceit that has led us to near-destruction."

"What is it you desire?" she demanded.

"I?" He ran a contented hand down the soft satin of
his black jacket. "What is mine by right. Dominion."

"Over humans?"

He grimaced. "I do not seek to rule mere fodder.
What are mortals to me? No. My dominion will be
over vampires. As is only proper."

Nefri narrowed her dark gaze. "The Great Council
will stop you. You cannot overcome them all."

Valkier offered a soft laugh. "A bothersome problem that you have at last allowed me to overcome, my
dear Nefri."

"The Medallion is beyond your reach," she warned.

"Ah yes, the precious Medallion." He folded his arms
over his chest, fully enjoying this moment of superiority over the woman who had spurned him. She would
learn that he was not a vampire to accept defeat. Not
ever. "I had hoped that my ruse would prove an adequate distraction for you and the Great Council."

"Distraction?"

"But of course." His smile was edged with a smug
satisfaction. "I realized that if I were to accomplish
my goals I must do something that would command
the complete attention of all vampires. What better
means than to threaten the precious Veil?" His smile
widened in a chilling fashion. "It was a simple matter to seduce the three fools into believing they
would soon possess the power of the Medallion. And

even simpler to persuade the Great Council to choose to send in defense those vampires who were so noble and filled with righteous self-worth that they would not merely dispose of the traitors, but actually attempt to save them from their own lusts. They provided all the diversion I required."

Oddly, the sadness about Nefri only seemed to deepen. The knowledge sent a surge of anger through Valkier. He wanted her frightened and begging for mercy, not regarding him with pity.

"And what did you hope to gain, Valkier?" she asked softly.

His hands curled as he battled the need to strike the flawless countenance. He would be respected. And feared.

"Unlike my brethren, I have not forgotten that the Medallion was only one of a pair," he retorted in smooth tones. "As with all ancient artifacts, it was made to provide a balance to the one who wielded the power. The eternal Yin and Yang. Darkness and light. Love and hatred. Creation and destruction." He slowly reached beneath his jacket to reveal the Medallion he had so recently stolen from Nefri's hidden lair. "You have quite foolishly chosen to divide the Medallion of Creation, lessening it to mere baubles. While I now possess the Medallion of Destruction."

The smooth expression never altered. "And what do you intend to do with it, Valkier?"

"It is quite simple. I intend to destroy the Veil and anyone who stands in my way."

There was a long silence before she stepped toward him, a slender hand outstretched.

"Do not do this, Valkier. You will only harm yourself."

His nose flared in fury. Why did she remain so calm? Why did she not plead for his mercy?

"Nothing can harm me now, Nefri. I am invincible."

"No, not invincible. The Medallion is a danger in itself."

"Do not speak." Valkier held up the Medallion, the wondrous glory he had expected to experience ruined by this woman who had plagued him for centuries. "You could have ruled at my side, Nefri. You could have been the Queen to my King. But instead you have chosen to oppose my will. For that you will be the first to feel my retribution. I fear I must say goodbye to you now. My destiny awaits."

Holding the Medallion high, Valkier felt the power cascade through his body with an intoxicating flood of pleasure. Soon, he moaned in painful arousal. Soon it would all be his.

Amelia was frozen in horror as she watched the two powerful vampires confront each other. Deep within her, a tiny voice whispered that she should do something. Surely she should at least run in search of Sebastian, or call out in warning?

But despite the frantic urge to help, she was bound by a paralyzing fear.

Instead she helplessly watched as Nefri squarely faced her assailant, her shabby disguise falling away to reveal a tall, proudly beautiful woman. She could sense no fear in the ancient vampire. Not even when Valkier revealed his evil intentions. Instead, there was an unmistakable pity that frightened Amelia even more.

It was obvious that Nefri had some feelings for the horrid intruder. Would such emotions keep her from protecting herself? Would she allow herself to be destroyed rather than strike out against this vampire who had clearly loved her at one time?

Struggling to find some means past the panic that

clutched at her, Amelia was abruptly distracted when the distinct sound of Sebastian's voice echoed in her mind.

Amelia.

Raising trembling fingers, she pressed them to her temple in confusion. "Sebastian?"

Yes, my dear.

"Where are you?"

Just beyond the trees.

Unnerved by the sensation of having his voice echoing within her mind, Amelia nevertheless swiftly concentrated upon the urgency of the situation.

"You must come. Nefri is in danger."

I know. I need you to come to me, Amelia. Try to move slowly and do not attract the attention of Valkier.

"But . . ."

Amelia, please. This is very important.

She attempted to swallow past the thick lump in her throat. "Very well."

Remember, be very careful.

"I will."

Pausing long enough to ensure that William remained sleeping peacefully upon the leather seat, Amelia gritted her teeth and began to inch her way through the door of the carriage. Her skirts briefly threatened to tangle between her legs, but she swiftly tugged them above her knees and poked the hem through the ribbon that tied beneath her bodice. This was no time for modesty.

Step by excruciatingly slow step, she reached the ground and began to slide along the length of the carriage. Her gaze never strayed from the cold, forbidding countenance of Valkier, but it was obvious that Nefri consumed him.

Still, she preferred to err upon the side of caution; ignoring the quivering muscles of her legs, she continued her crab-like steps until she was well away from the vampires. Only then did she breathe in deeply and allow herself to sense where Sebastian awaited.

He was closer than she had expected, and not alone. With a frown of concern, she ducked low and dodged her way through the edge of the trees. Had Drake followed Sebastian? Did he even now hold him hostage? Was that why he had called to her?

Her pace hastened until she at last forced her way through a deep thicket and stumbled forward to find Sebastian impatiently awaiting her.

"Amelia."

With satisfying swiftness, she found herself swept into a fierce embrace as Sebastian pressed a kiss to her lips and only reluctantly pulled back to study her.

"Sebastian." Her hands gripped the lapels of his coat, as much to keep her upright as to keep him close. "What has happened? Did you capture Drake?"

He gave a pained grimace. "No. He was destroyed before I could reach him."

"Destroyed?" Her eyes widened. "How?"

"Valkier. He must have been awaiting him the moment he left the cottage. I tried to follow the trail of the slayer, but it was impossible."

She shuddered at the thought of the dreadful vampire who even now threatened Nefri. "Oh, Sebastian, he is near the carriage. He is determined to harm Nefri."

"Yes. We must stop him." He managed a faint smile as he gave her shoulders a reassuring squeeze. "Thankfully, Nefri seemingly suspected the truth about Valkier and was wise enough to take steps in case he attacked."

Amelia frowned. "What steps?"

Moving to one side, Sebastian waved a slender hand toward the silent forms that stood in the shadows. Just for a moment, Amelia remained puzzled. There were two gentlemen, one tall with an arrogant beauty about him, and the other a golden-haired rogue with a smile that could melt the most impervious female heart. There were also two women, both outrageously lovely, although one possessed a cold, Nordic fairness and the other was blessed with a serene charm with raven curls and deep blue eyes.

It was not until she noted the matching golden amulets that hung about the women's necks that realization struck. These were Sebastian's brothers and the maidens they had been sent to protect.

"Amelia, may I introduce you to Gideon and his wife Simone? And Lucien, who has recently wed Jocelyn."

There was a muted greeting before Amelia returned her attention to the vampire at her side.

"What is occurring?"

"Nefri summoned Gideon and Lucien to bring their brides to the cottage," he explained.

"But why? Are we to battle Valkier?"

"Only in a manner of speaking." Sebastian held her gaze steadily, his expression somber. "I must have your amulet, Amelia."

She blinked in surprise at his request. "Why?"

The tall, rather arrogant vampire stepped forward. "The Medallion must be made whole again. It is the only means of stopping Valkier."

"Oh." Amelia searched Sebastian's face for the answers to her lingering questions.

He offered a reassuring glance. "The Medallions are a pair, each with their own powers and each able to hold the other in balance. We must return your Medallion to Nefri if we are to save her."

Amelia was still uncertain what powers he spoke of, but she did not hesitate to tug the necklace over her head. She would do anything she could to halt the horrid Valkier.

With absolute trust, she placed the amulet in Sebastian's hand, rather surprised when Simone and Jocelyn appeared at her side to add their own amulets.

For a moment there was nothing but the odd glow that was always a part of the amulets. But even as she wondered what was supposed to occur, the glow brightened, limning Sebastian's body in a blazing light. Amelia narrowed her gaze against the abrupt flash of light, stepping back instinctively.

"Sebastian," she cried softly, terrified that he was being injured.

Thankfully, the light vanished as swiftly as it had burst to life. She met Sebastian's reassuring glance.

"All is well, Amelia." He held out his hand to reveal the Medallion, once again made whole. "Now, remain here. Gideon, Lucien, and I must take this to Nefri."

Opening her mouth to protest, Amelia stopped when she was firmly flanked by the two women, both wearing expressions as stubborn as her own.

"We will be going as well," Simone said in a soft but determined tone.

Soft laughter echoed through the trees as Gideon and Lucien shared rueful glances. Then, with a shake of his head, the golden-haired rogue moved toward the frowning Sebastian.

"Do not seek to argue, my old friend," Lucien advised in a twinkling glance toward his wife. "A wise vampire avoids those battles that he is destined to lose. Especially when that battle is with the woman who shares his bed."

Sebastian appeared less than pleased by the thought of Amelia placing herself in danger, but with a sharp nod of his head he began weaving his way through the trees. Gideon and Lucien were swiftly following in his path. Amelia, along with her staunch allies, brought up the rear.

In silence they moved back toward Nefri and the forbidding Valkier. Amelia shivered as the thick feeling of bleak hatred threatened to overwhelm her. In truth she had no desire to continue onward. What possible help could she be? She had no means to overcome the obviously crazed vampire or even to offer Nefri any assistance.

But there was no chance that she was going to allow Sebastian to be in the presence of the deadly Valkier without her near. No matter how her heart might quail or her knees threaten to buckle.

Grimly she fought to keep her feet moving forward, only halting when Lucien turned to hold up a warning hand. On cue, all three women crouched in the overgrowth and turned their attention toward the two vampires locked in their private war of wills.

Amelia tightly clutched the hands of her companions as the three gentlemen continued forward, Sebastian taking the lead as he hid the Medallion in his clenched hand. Her heart nearly came to a full stop as Valkier abruptly spun to confront the intruders. Dear heavens, she had never seen eyes that glittered with such a lethal intent or features so lacking in emotion. She knew beyond a doubt that he would cut down his brothers without a hint of regret.

He would destroy anything or anyone who stood in his path.

"Ah, Sebastian, you have invited companions. What a charming surprise," the gaunt-faced vampire drawled, his flat gaze flickering over the large figures stalking ever closer. "I did not dare to hope that I would have witnesses in my moment of glory. You shall be the first to bow to my authority."

"Never," Sebastian snapped, not even flinching beneath the deadly glare.

A cold laugh swept through the air. "Do not be any more of a fool than necessary, Sebastian. You were nearly bested by the pitiable Drake. I have command of the Medallion. You cannot hope to stand against me."

Sebastian never wavered. "I do not fear you, Valkier."

"You should." The vampire lifted the heavy Medallion, smiling as the malevolent radiance filled the shadows. "There are few things that I shall enjoy more than ridding our world of such spineless wretches." His eyes narrowed. "To know you have willingly bonded with mortals is nauseating. You have defiled all vampires with your animal lusts."

Amelia cried out in alarm, but before anyone could react, Nefri was standing in front of Sebastian, her expression stern.

"No, Valkier. This must not happen. The Medallion was never meant to be used in such a manner."

The vampire gave a low snarl. "The power is mine. No one can deny me what is rightfully my destiny. You should have stood at my side, Nefri. Now you must be destroyed."

"Valkier . . ."

Nefri's plea went unheeded as the vampire abruptly unleashed his power. Amelia's eyes widened in horror as the sickening glow flared out with a bluish glare. Sebastian and his companions were suddenly engulfed, disappearing in the foul light.

"Sebastian, no," Amelia breathed.

Frantic to reach his side, she struggled to her feet only to be ruthlessly pulled back behind the bush by the women she had thought were her champions.

"Wait," Jocelyn whispered close to her ear. "Have faith in Sebastian."

Amelia trembled with fear. Faith? She did not desire to have faith. She wanted to rush forward and vanquish the horrid vampire with her bare hands. The women, however, refused to loosen their fierce grip, and she was forced to watch in helpless terror.

The glow deepened, pulsing in an ominous fashion. Amelia moaned in despair, certain that the end was near; then, abruptly, Valkier's eyes widened and a keening cry was wrenched from his throat.

"No . . . it is impossible. No."

The cry became a bloodcurdling scream and in shocked disbelief, Amelia watched as his thin frame began to tremble with unnatural force. For what seemed an eternity, Valkier screamed in horrific agony, and just when Amelia became convinced that she could bear no more, the vampire began to blacken as if being burned from within.

Nauseated by the ghastly scene before her, Amelia turned her head aside. Whatever her disgust for the arrogant, avaricious Valkier, she could not bear to witness his end.

Battling the rising bile, it took long moments for her to realize that a deep, wounded silence had filled the copse. Indeed, she did not even sense Sebastian's approach until she was being gently pulled into his arms.

"It is over, Amelia," he said in weary tones.

With an effort she lifted her head to regard him with tear-filled eyes. "How?"

It was Nefri who answered as she gently bent over the burned ashes that lay upon the damp ground.

"It was the Medallion," she said softly, her voice hoarse with regret. "The powers were intended to balance one another. To attempt to gain dominance caused the Medallion to turn itself against Valkier. He should have known. Above all, harmony must be maintained."

Shamelessly clutching Sebastian close to her, Amelia burrowed her head in his shoulder.

"It is truly over?"

"Yes, my love." She felt his lips lightly brush the top of her hair. "And now I think it is time to go home."

Home. A slow, wondrous smile curved her lips as she breathed deeply of his warm, familiar scent. Yes. That is what she now possessed. A home. Complete with the man who would be at her side for all eternity.

Epilogue

The wedding of Sebastian and Amelia a fortnight later was intended to be a quiet affair.

With her parents stiffly declining her invitation to join her in London, and her handful of acquaintances having turned their back on her the moment she had left society, Amelia had no one but William and Mrs. Benson to be her witnesses.

She pretended that it did not matter. After all, she and Sebastian were already as one. His every thought, his every heartbeat, was a part of her. The ceremony was a mere formality; they were already indeed man and wife.

That, and, of course, a prelude to the wedding night . . .

With a philosophical determination, Amelia kept her thoughts centered upon that pleasant eventuality. She was desperately hungry for the moment Sebastian would at last carry her to the chambers he had refurbished so thoughtfully. His every touch had only intensified her searing desire for him.

A desperation she easily sensed echoed within Sebastian.

The knowledge that she had found her true mate was far more important than a gaggle of curious onlookers, she sternly reminded herself.

Tossing herself into the effort to change the town house from a shrouded mausoleum to something resembling a home, Amelia managed to appear as happy and carefree as any bride-to-be. Even during the brief wedding ceremony and the drive back to their home, Amelia was certain that she had managed to conceal any hint of regret.

It was a certainty that was destroyed the moment Sebastian happily carried her over the threshold and into the front parlor that was filled with guests. In amazement, Amelia had noted several unfamiliar faces that she was certain must be vampires, and, of course, Lucien and Gideon along with their smiling wives.

Her eyes filled with happiness as she glanced up to meet her husband's tender gaze.

He had, of course, known all along. And with his usual efficiency had managed to provide precisely what she desired. Indifferent to the numerous eyes upon them, Amelia pulled his head downward to kiss him with all the love that flowed through her heart.

Loud cheers and clapping at last brought her to her senses, and with decidedly warm cheeks she loosened her grip upon her husband to meet his glittering gaze.

"Welcome home, Mrs. St. Ives," he said softly.

"What did you do with all the dust covers?" she teased as a profound sense of joy bloomed within her heart. The parlor had been one room she had not yet reached with her ruthless refurbishing.

"Do not fear, my dear. I have kept them quite handy so we can replace them the moment we have rid ourselves of these bothersome guests."

Her brows lifted in surprise. "Replace them? Why on earth would we do that?"

The silver eyes glowed with a decidedly wicked light. "Now that you are most certainly mine, Mrs.

St. Ives, I intend to keep you far too occupied to concern yourself with entertaining."

Her laughter tinkled through the room. "Why, Mr. St. Ives, is that any way for a proper, always dignified scholar to behave?"

"Well, as a scholar I have always forced myself to know all there is about a subject before coming to a conclusion." His gaze lowered with an aching desire to the fullness of her lips. "You are going to require a most thorough and continuing examination, I fear."

"A most fascinating proposal," she murmured softly.

With a growl he pressed a quick, searing kiss to her lips before reluctantly lowering her to her feet.

"Go enjoy your guests, my love," he husked close to her ear, "before I have them thrown onto the curb."

She reached up to lightly touch his lean cheek. "Patience, Sebastian. We have an eternity together."

His gaze briefly lowered to where the amulet had been returned to the chain about her neck. A smile of pure contentment curved his full lips.

"An eternity. Yes. That should perhaps be just long enough to show you how much I love you."

ABOUT THE AUTHOR

Debbie Raleigh lives with her family in Missouri. Debbie loves to hear from readers, and you may write to her c/o Zebra Books. Please include a self-addressed stamped envelope if you wish a response.